Hardy Boys Mystery Stories

THE WAILING SIREN MYSTERY

BY

FRANKLIN W. DIXON

NEW YORK
GROSSET & DUNLAP
Publishers

CONTENTS

THE WAILING SIREN MYSTERY

CHAPTER I

Money from the Sky

THE *Sleuth* roared toward Barmet Bay as fast as its propeller could churn the sullen sea. At its wheel sat Joe Hardy, tensely watching the black clouds. His brother Frank bent anxiously over the throbbing motor.

"Think we'll make it?" Joe asked.

"If the engine holds out. Listen! It's missing again!"

The motor coughed. At the same time a jagged bolt of lightning flung itself from a towering thunderhead. It was followed by a deafening crash. As rain poured down on the boys in blinding sheets, the engine suddenly conked out.

"We're in for it!" Frank called.

"What's the matter?"

"It could be the gas line."

Frank flung open the hatch to the engine, grabbed

the toolbox, and set to work. Without power, the *Sleuth* was in danger of being capsized by the giant waves.

"I'll try to keep her heading into the wind," Joe shouted. He turned the wheel back and forth in an effort to avoid sliding into a trough.

The storm had broken in all its fury. Lightning flashed almost continuously, and the air reverberated to the roll of thunder. One blinding flash came very near the boat.

"Wow!" Joe exclaimed. "A little closer and we would have had it!"

"Never saw a storm come up so fast," Frank said.

The brothers, high school boys out for an evening cruise in their motorboat, had gone farther onto the ocean from Barmet Bay than usual. Dark-haired Frank, tall, slender, and keen-witted, was worried. Joe, a year younger, with blond, wavy hair and an impetuous nature, was not too concerned as yet.

This trait of Joe's was responsible for their present predicament. Joe had listened to only the first half of the late afternoon weather report. At the end, the announcer had told of the possibility of a storm. Now the brothers were caught in the center of a heavy summer squall.

Frothy whitecaps slapped over the side of the boat, which rocked dangerously in the turbulent sea. Despite the ponchos that the boys had grabbed out of a locker, their trousers and feet were becoming soaked.

They thought little of this. What did worry Frank was that the Barmet Bay inlet, with its blinking beacons, seemed to be drifting away from the *Sleuth* at a fearful rate.

"How's it coming?" Joe called.

"No luck yet. If this storm keeps up, Mother'll be a wreck. You know how she worries about us being out here in bad weather."

"And Aunt Gertrude isn't helping her any," Joe added. "She's probably telling Mother of the perils of the sea and why boys shouldn't have motorboats."

"I wish Dad were home to calm them. Did he say when he was coming back from Washington?"

"No," Joe replied. "He never can tell how long his secret government cases are going to last."

"I wonder what it's about this time? He said we might be of some help to him in—"

Frank was interrupted by another large wave which caught the bow of the *Sleuth* with a resounding *whack*. It pitched Frank off balance. Joe clung to the wheel.

"A couple more like that and we'll be swamped!" Frank shouted.

By this time the waves had become so towering that the motorboat shuddered under each impact.

The rain cut against the faces of the brothers like handfuls of sharp sand.

As Joe pulled hard on the wheel to avoid an avalanche of water, he cried out, "Frank, look!"

"What?"

"Over there. That ship!"

In the distance a yacht was bobbing up and down in the giant waves.

"Maybe the captain'll help us out," Frank suggested. "Let's signal."

He picked up a flashlight and beamed an S O S, hoping to attract attention. There was no response. The *Sleuth* was evidently too low in the water for the signal to be seen.

In a matter of minutes it was completely dark on the water. The lightning and thunder ceased, but rain continued to fall and the wind to blow.

The motor of the *Sleuth* was still dead. Frank had been unable to locate the trouble with the craft rocking so violently. The use of tools was out of the question.

Suddenly Joe shouted. "Frank, the yacht's heading this way. We'll be run down!"

Frantically he signaled with his flash. A moment later the winking lights of the ship were blotted out. Why had they been extinguished?

Hearts beating wildly, the boys waited. If the ship came closer without seeing them, there would be only one thing for them to do—jump overboard! They listened frantically for the sound of its approach.

Suddenly the brothers saw the yacht's lights again. They were farther away than before.

"Whew!" said Frank in relief.

"I think I hear a plane coming," Joe said. "Let's signal again."

Both boys strained to hear its sound. Above the roar of the wind and the breakers came the steady drone of a motor.

"That pilot's crazy to be out in a storm like this," said Joe.

"Maybe he's lost," Frank suggested. "From the sound, he must be circling. But I can't see him."

"Nor I. Hope he doesn't think the light on the yacht is a landing field," Joe said with a shudder. "If he comes down on top of us, we're goners!"

At that moment a wailing sound filled the air. It was like the warning siren of an ambulance in action.

"Where's that coming from?" Joe exclaimed.

"Either the plane or the yacht," Frank reasoned. "The sound wouldn't carry this far from shore in the storm."

The yacht's deck lights blazed again. Then as before they disappeared.

"What's going on?" Joe asked.

"Wish I knew."

Clear vision was cut off by the blinding rain. Five minutes, ten minutes went by. The plane's motor could be heard faintly.

Then suddenly its drone became clearer again. Within a matter of seconds the craft was directly overhead. As the boys looked up, there was a swishing sound, then a smack on the water directly alongside the *Sleuth*. Leaning way over, Frank reached out and just managed to grasp an object as it was about to sink beneath the waves.

"What is it?" Joe asked.

"Feels like a wallet! And a fat one, too."

Flashing his light on the billfold, Frank whistled. "It's full of money!"

CHAPTER II

Two Losses

JOE'S eyes popped at sight of the bulging wallet. "It must have dropped from the plane, but why, is more than I can figure out," he muttered.

Frank flashed his light and exclaimed, "Hundred-dollar bills!" As he started to count them, Joe suddenly shouted, "Hang on!"

A big wave was bearing down on them. It hit the craft broadside, tilting it and throwing Frank and Joe into the churning water. Automatically they struggled out of their ponchos.

The wave was followed in rapid succession by two smaller ones. No sooner had they surfaced than they were hit immediately by the oncoming walls of water.

Despite the predicament they were in, Frank and Joe kept their heads. Being sons of Fenton Hardy, the famous detective, they had been well schooled in meeting perilous situations.

Starting with their adventure involving the mystery of *The Tower Treasure*, they had had many narrow escapes tracking down criminals. Their latest case, known as *The Secret of the Lost Tunnel*, had taken them to the South on the trail of Civil War gold. But now they realized that the elements could be as dangerous as the craftiest of criminals.

The sturdy motorboat rose tantalizingly out of their reach on a huge wave. Spluttering and struggling, Frank and Joe fought their way toward the *Sleuth*. Though excellent swimmers, they had all they could do to overtake it.

Joe was the first to grasp the side of the boat. With eyes smarting and head spinning, he lifted himself over the gunwale.

Then Frank grabbed hold. He hoisted one leg over the side and tumbled into the bottom of the boat.

"Did—did you lose the wallet?" Joe asked.

Frank held up the dripping wallet, still clutched in one hand. The leather was well worn, but a quick flip showed the money was still there. They would count it later. Frank put it in his pocket.

The rain had stopped, and visibility was better. The yacht was now in sight, but moving rapidly southward.

"It made a quick getaway," Frank remarked. "Wonder where it's going."

While Joe bailed out the boat with a large can from the locker, Frank continued his work on the motor. Finally he found the trouble—the gas line. He repaired it quickly with skillful fingers.

"Try the starter, Joe."

The motor roared into action. One danger was over, although it would still be no child's play to make the inlet.

Frank wiped his hands on some waste. "It's all yours, skipper." He had the utmost confidence in his brother, who knew every inch of the coast along Barmet Bay.

"I'm sure curious about that wallet," Joe said as they plowed along through the stormy sea.

"I think I'll count it." Frank beamed his flash on the bills and thumbed through them.

"How much?" Joe asked eagerly.

"Two thousand dollars!" Frank exclaimed. "And not a mark of identification in the wallet."

Joe grinned. "We'll have a sweet time finding the owner."

"He might not want to be found," Frank said slowly. "Maybe it's stolen money."

"What makes you think so?"

"Looks as if there had once been an owner's card under this cellophane. A corner of it's still here."

The boys continued to speculate about the wallet

until they neared the mouth of the inlet. Then conversation ceased while Joe put all his energy into the task of keeping the *Sleuth* on a straight course.

Whenever the sea was high, a dangerous whirl-pool swirled near the inlet. Joe took a bearing on the blinker of the entrance buoy, and skirted the churning water. In five minutes they were riding smoothly. The turbulent ocean was behind them!

"Neat navigating!" Frank commented, as he saw the lights of Bayport twinkle in the distance.

When the *Sleuth* finally came alongside the dock where the Hardy boys kept their boat, Joe cut the motor. Frank leaped ashore and secured the line.

Two men hurried toward him. Frank recognized them at once as Detective Smuff and Patrolman Con Riley of the Bayport Police Department.

"Where have you two been?" Smuff shouted.

"Out in the *Sleuth*," Frank replied. "Why?"

Smuff turned to Riley. "He asks me why. That's what you call gratitude! We've been looking for these boys two hours and he asks me why!"

Frank slipped Joe a look. "Why were you look-ing for us? Anything wrong at home?"

"No," said Riley. "But see here, you've been lost. Didn't you know it?"

The boys grinned. They had had dealings with these men before. They were veteran members of the local police force, both well-meaning men, but not distinguished for their powers of imagination or deduction.

"Why didn't you take the police launch and hunt for us?" Frank asked.

"That's the Coast Guard's business, son, and after that last run-in with them, we know better than to interfere," replied Officer Riley.

Smuff did not seem to be paying attention. He stood beneath a dock light jotting something down in a small notebook.

"Found—Hardy—boys—in—bay," he read aloud. "Now that'll sound okay on the blotter, eh, Riley?"

"You didn't find us," Joe said.

"Oh, yes, we did," Smuff insisted. "We spotted you in the boat just before you landed."

"Who sent out the alarm for us?" Frank asked anxiously.

"Your mother."

"Lock up our gear, Joe, while I telephone home," Frank directed.

He ran halfway down the block to a drugstore. After telephoning Mrs. Hardy that they were safe, he hurried back to Joe, then the brothers drove home in their coupé which they had left in a parking lot.

Mrs. Hardy flung open the front door and hugged her sons as they came in. She was a petite woman, with a pretty face and wavy hair. Frank and Joe bent down to kiss her.

"Thank goodness you're safe," she exclaimed.

"It was rough going for a while," Joe said, putting an arm around his mother's shoulder. "But it was worth it. We ran into what may turn out to be a big mystery."

"What was that? Another mystery?" The voice belonged to Aunt Gertrude, unmarried sister of Mr. Hardy, who lived at their home. She came bustling down the stairs. "Well, you're not going to have anything to do with it!"

Tall, angular Aunt Gertrude was a very energetic person. She felt that her chief mission in life was to protect her nephews from the dangers involved in their mysteries, especially when their father was away from home.

While the boys changed into dry clothes, Mrs. Hardy prepared a meal of sandwiches and milk. As they ate, Aunt Gertrude plied them with questions about the mystery. They told of their strange experience during the storm—the yacht that had vanished so suddenly, the plane, the wailing siren, and finally the wallet.

Frank went upstairs for it. When he laid the water-soaked contents on the table, Mrs. Hardy and Aunt Gertrude gasped in amazement.

"Two thousand dollars!"

"And it fell right out of the sky with no identification," Frank explained.

"Nothing good will come of this," Aunt Gertrude predicted. "That's bad money. I just know it is. Frank, get rid of it right away. We're likely to have some cutthroat come here to recover it."

"I think Aunt Gertrude's idea about not keeping the money here is a good one," said Mrs. Hardy. "I wish your father were home to advise us what to do."

"How about our taking the wallet to police headquarters?" Frank suggested.

"I think you should," Mrs. Hardy agreed.

The boys hurried to the station house. They found Smuff and Riley reporting to Police Chief Collig the rescue of the Hardys. The chief's eyes showed surprise when he saw the boys.

"I—I thought you two were nearly dead from drowning!" he exclaimed.

Joe grinned. "We Hardys revive quickly."

Smuff and Riley left in a hurry, and the boys spoke to the chief alone, telling about the wallet.

"We thought we'd better leave it here for safekeeping," Frank explained.

The chief said he would send out a teletype notice of "a large sum of money found near Bayport," and hoped for a quick response. Curious to hear whether the teletype message had brought forth any claimants, Frank telephoned him after breakfast next morning. Nobody had inquired about the money.

Joe suggested that the brothers drive to the Bayport airfield. Perhaps some pilot had reported dropping a wallet. On reaching the administration building there, Frank asked the man at the desk if any flier had mentioned losing anything from a plane the night before.

"Last night, you say? No planes were up in that storm."

"We heard one."

"It wasn't from here," the man said. "And no one landed during the storm."

The boys telephoned two other airports in the vicinity, receiving the same answer. No known planes were in flight at the time the wallet was dropped. As the Hardys drove back to the city, Frank said:

"It's my guess the plane was a private one."

"That still doesn't explain why the wallet fell out," Joe mused. "And it's pretty certain the owner wouldn't expect to recover the money from the ocean. What do you think we ought to do about it?"

"I think it's our duty to put an ad in the newspaper," Frank replied. "Let's stop at the *News* on the way home."

When they reached the office of the *Bayport News*, Frank scratched a few lines on a sheet of paper and handed them to the classified ad clerk. They read:

Found: Wallet near Bayport. Contains sum of money. Owner identify and write Q.E.D., Box 22, News Office.

"I hope this lands the real owner," Joe said on the way home, "and not a lot of phonies."

The boys had been home only long enough to eat lunch when they heard somebody run up the front porch steps. A second later their bell rang frantically and a fist pounded on the door.

Frank opened it. The boys' overweight friend Chet Morton raced in. From his flushed face and heaving chest it appeared as if he had run a long distance.

"Frank! Joe!" he shouted. "You've got to help me quick!"

"What's the matter?"

"We've been robbed! Somebody stole our truck! All my uncle's rifles were in it!"

CHAPTER III

Telltale Tracks

THE HARDYS learned that in the absence of Mr. Morton, Chet had gone to the railroad station in the farm truck to pick up a box of high-powered rifles. These guns, on special order by Tyler Morton, Chet's uncle and famous big-game hunter, had been sent by a New England gunsmith to the express office in Bayport.

"Uncle Ty's coming to our place in two weeks to get his stuff ready for a trip to Africa," Chet explained. "But now his plans will be ruined. His guns are gone!"

"How come? Where was the truck?" Frank asked, instantly eager for details.

Chet said he had loaded the big box onto the truck and then had driven to the Wells Hardware Company to pick up a chest of tools his father had ordered.

"While I was at the store," Chet continued, "I

picked out a lot of camping equipment I knew we would need for our trip." Sheepishly he added, "I picked out a dandy canoe, too."

"Did you pay for all this stuff?" Joe queried.

"No. Charged it. I thought if you didn't like the stuff, I could return it." Chet put his head in his hands and moaned. "If I don't get 'em back, I'll have to pay for 'em all!"

"Pretty tough," Frank remarked. "Then what happened?"

"Everything was loaded into the back of the truck," Chet explained. "I started to drive home. But I was hungry."

"So you stopped for a sandwich," Joe guessed.

Chet said that was exactly what he had done. He had pulled into the Pines, a roadside eating place.

"I only had a couple of three-deckers," the plump youth explained. "When I went outside for the truck, it—it was gone."

"You left the keys in it?" Joe asked, frowning.

"Yes."

"How long ago did this happen?" Frank asked. "We'd better get busy. Did you notify the police, Chet?"

"No. I came right here."

Chet was so flustered he could not remember the license number of the truck. Frank telephoned

Chief Collig what had happened. Then he sped out of the house with Chet and Joe, and took the wheel of the boys' coupé.

"We'll start from the Pines," he said.

There was silence for a few seconds, then Joe asked, "Why did you buy all that camping stuff, Chet?"

"We were talking about a trip, weren't we?"

"Nothing was definite."

"I know," Chet admitted.

When they arrived at the restaurant, Chet showed the other boys the spot where the truck had been parked.

"Are these marks in the mud from your tires?" Joe asked.

Chet nodded. "Yes. They're plain enough, because those rear tires were new."

The brothers easily traced the tracks to the road, where they learned that the truck had headed north. Quickly returning to their car, the boys drove in the same direction.

Frank continued along the highway for nearly two miles, slowing down at each intersection to see if there were any tire marks along the soft sides of the roadway, showing that the missing truck had turned off. The highway skirted Bayport, then continued north through rolling woods and farm lands.

Several miles out, at a dirt crossroad, Frank

stopped to look at some tire prints on the left fork. After a careful examination, he shouted:

"I see them!" He knelt on one knee at the right side of the road, pointing to some impressions in the dirt. "But say, another car followed right in the truck's tracks. Wonder if that means anything."

Chet was not listening. "Come on," he shouted.

They hopped into the car. Frank turned left and followed the country road. It wound downward through the soft earth to a deep gully, then up the other side to the top of a sparsely wooded hill. The double tracks continued for some distance, then suddenly became only one set of tire marks.

"Now what?" Frank asked, perplexed. "The truck didn't go any farther."

Joe jumped out. Reason told him the truck had turned off, but where? There was no side road.

"It—it just couldn't happen," Chet moaned.

In a moment Joe began tearing at some bushes along the road. His trained eye had noted they were wilting; probably torn up a little while before and piled there as a screen.

"Look!" he shouted, pulling the bushes away.

A corduroy road, its timbers rotting, forked from the dirt highway—a lumberman's road, long-since deserted when the stand of timber had been cut. Weeds that grew up between the logs clearly showed the two crushed trails that the wheels had made.

"Wait here," said Joe.

He disappeared into the woods, but returned in a couple of minutes.

"I found your truck, Chet," he said.

"Hoo–ray!" Chet shouted. "Gee, that's super! Now Uncle Ty can go to Africa and we can take that camping trip!"

"The truck is empty!"

"Honest?" Chet's jaw dropped.

Frank had an idea. "I believe that the other car was following on purpose. The driver was a pal of the truck thief. They must have known about this wood road where they could work without being seen."

"And loaded the guns, tools, and camping stuff into the car and drove off," Joe said. "A stolen truck's hard to get rid of, but loot isn't."

"What about the canoe?" Frank asked.

"It could have been fastened to the roof. A lot of cars have ski racks up on top, you know," Joe replied.

Chet was in a quandary. Chasing a truck thief was bad enough, but going after two desperate men with a lot of rifles in their possession was more than he had bargained for.

"I guess we'd better let the police handle this," he said.

"What! Let those thieves get away now, when

we're on their trail!" Joe cried. "I'll back the truck out," he offered, "and then we'll go after 'em!"

With Chet's help he maneuvered the truck onto the dirt road, then trailed Frank and Chet for a mile and a half. During the ride Chet was told about the wallet the Hardys had found.

"Wow!" Chet exclaimed. "Two thousand dollars!"

Frank stopped suddenly. Joe pulled up in the truck right behind him and jumped out.

"Trail end?" he asked.

"No. But the car stopped here and backed up to the side of the road," Frank replied. "See these marks?"

"Good eyesight to catch that," Joe said admiringly. He began to investigate and concluded that the loot might have been carried into the woods at this point. Bushes were beaten down here and there, and near the edge of a brook footprints were clearly visible. The boys searched up and downstream, but no further trace of the thieves could be found.

"No point in going any deeper in the woods," Frank said. "We're only guessing that the stolen stuff is here. Anyway, this is North Woods." He winked at Joe. "You know what that means."

Chet's eyes bulged. "You mean the place where people say they've heard wild dogs?"

"The same," Frank nodded. "And a wild dog is as mean as a wolf."

"I don't want to meet any of 'em," Chet said.

"Not even to get the stolen stuff back?"

"Let the police find it," Chet advised. "And if they don't . . . Say, you fellows got all that money. How about letting me have some of it to pay for the stolen rifles and everything?"

"Not on your life," Joe replied, laughing. "It doesn't belong to us." He winked at Frank. "I'm afraid you'll have to earn the money to pay for the stuff, Chet."

Chet groaned. He realized now that it had been a mistake to order the camping equipment without the Hardys' consent. Too often in his life he had made similar unfortunate mistakes and had had to pay for them with hard work, to which he was allergic.

The Hardys returned to their car. This time Chet drove the truck. Twenty minutes later they came to the intersecting macadam road, Black Horse Pike, where they lost the trail.

"We'd better report to the police that we found the truck," Frank said, as they headed back to Bayport.

A couple of miles farther on they came to a state police substation. Frank went in. After telling the desk sergeant of the recovery of the truck, he reported that a box of valuable big game rifles, a set of tools, a canoe, and other camping equipment had been removed from it.

The sergeant, a tall, broad-shouldered man, frowned. "High-powered rifles are dangerous weapons to be in the hands of criminals," he said. "We'll make a careful search for the stuff right away."

When the Hardys arrived home, they found their school friends Biff Hooper and Tony Prito waiting for them. Biff was a tall, lanky boy whose chief delight was his secondhand jeep, while Tony, olive-skinned and dark-eyed, could usually be found around Barmet Bay, racing his bright red motor-boat, the *Napoli*.

"Hi, fellows!" Joe called out.

"What about our camping trip?" Biff asked. "Made any plans?"

"I think we ought to postpone the long trip we had in mind," Frank said. "Let's go to North Woods this week end instead." He told about the theft of Mr. Morton's truck and the things in it.

"You mean you want us to search North Woods for the rifles and other stuff?" Tony asked.

"That's right."

"If there's anything to those stories about wild dogs out there, we'd better not take any chances," Biff suggested.

"I don't think there's a thing to the rumor," Tony scoffed.

After mapping plans for the week-end trip, Biff and Tony left. Joe telephoned Chet to ask him to join them. His whistle of alarm at the thought of going into North Woods came piercingly over the telephone wire.

"Okay, if you don't want to go," said Joe. "But it's your stuff that was stolen. What are you going to tell your uncle?"

"You win." Chet sighed. "I'll go."

After an early supper Joe busied himself getting out their sleeping bags. Frank hurried downtown to the newspaper office. There was a remote chance, he thought, that somebody already had answered the ad about the mysterious wallet.

The clerk on duty, a high school friend who worked there during the evening, hailed Frank as he entered the building.

"Say," he said, "a stranger left a letter in your box a few minutes ago."

He handed the envelope to Frank, who tore it open eagerly. Then he frowned. The message was brief and mystifying.

Don't give the money to anyone until you hear from me again.

The strange note was signed "Rainy Night."

CHAPTER IV

Followed!

"WHAT did the man look like, Ken?" Frank asked excitedly.

The clerk grinned. "Another Hardy mystery, I'll bet. Well, this fellow was short and dark. Had a slight limp. Worc dark glasses."

Frank suspected the stranger might have worn the glasses as a partial disguise. "Did you notice anything special about them?" he asked.

Ken shook his head, then a second later said, "A piece of the frame was broken off."

"Which eye?"

"Listen, Frank, I'm no detective."

"Think!" Frank commanded. "It's important."

"Okay, teacher. I guess it was the left eye," he said slowly, as he tried to remember.

"That's swell. Thanks, Ken. It will help a lot."

"Want me to call the cops if he returns?" the clerk asked.

"I'm sure that won't be necessary. Something tells me that man won't show up here again."

Frank said this loud enough to be heard by several persons standing near the counter. Out of the corner of his eye he watched for any sign of interest, in case the mysterious fellow with the dark glasses might have a pal posted to watch. A man who had his back turned seemed to be listening. Could he be the accomplice?

Frank decided that if the man or anyone else was a confederate, he would probably follow him out of the newspaper office.

"Somebody ought to follow *him*," Frank thought.

Moving quietly to a telephone booth at one end of the office, he quickly dialed his home. Lowering his voice to make sure no one could overhear him, he said:

"Joe?"

"Yes, Frank, what's up?"

"I'm at the *News* office. A strange note was left for us. I think that the man who wrote it or a pal of his may try to follow me. Come down and watch, will you?"

"Right."

Frank stepped from the booth and resumed his conversation with his friend Ken. In a few minutes he noticed Joe walk past the door. Shortly afterward Frank said good night to the clerk and ambled out.

A woman who had been thumbing through some back issues in the newspaper file immediately stopped what she was doing and started after the boy. She wore a hat which shaded her face most effectively, so that Frank could not distinguish her features.

Frank lingered a moment in front of the building to look at some photos in the display window. The woman crossed the street and went into a store.

As Frank started on, a tall, blond-haired man, intently reading a newspaper which partially concealed his face, emerged from the store and took the same direction as Frank.

Reflected in a glass store front across the street was Joe, who was following at a discreet distance. Frank tried to act as though he was unhurried. The man, looking up from his paper, but keeping his face turned as if still looking in the shopwindows, followed at the same gait.

Frank walked faster. So did the man. A few moments later Frank looked back. To his dismay he saw that the woman was now following Joe!

"Do they know we are the ones who found the money, and are on our trail?" Frank wondered.

He turned from South Street into Market Street.

Glancing over his shoulder a few seconds later, he noticed that no one else had rounded the corner. Frank retraced his steps, gazing here and there on the sidewalk as if he had dropped something. Joe, the man, and the woman had vanished.

Frank peered down side streets and through open doorways. There was no sign of any of them. He was just beginning to feel a little worried, when far down the block he saw Joe suddenly wave at him.

Frank halted while Joe caught up. "Where'd they go?" Frank asked. "And where have you been?"

"Chasing 'em."

Joe reported that he had heard a whistle behind him. Turning, he had seen the woman. Both she and the man had ducked into a service driveway and disappeared.

"Sure seems as if they're working together," Frank commented. "I wonder if they've stopped following us."

"Let's hope so," said Joe. "Too bad I didn't get a good look at that man's face."

His brother nodded. "If those people are after the two thousand dollars we found, they'll try something else to learn who has it."

"Maybe I was dumb to signal you," Joe said. "That man and woman probably are watching us right now."

The brothers decided to separate and take zigzag routes home in order to throw any possible pursuers off the track. Fifteen minutes later they reached the house. For nearly an hour they discussed the affair with their mother and aunt.

"It's a good thing you shook those brassy creatures," Aunt Gertrude declared. "Why, they might have murdered us all in our beds. And to no avail, either, with the money locked up at the police station."

Next morning, as the boys were eating breakfast with Mrs. Hardy, Aunt Gertrude, who had been out for an early morning walk, bustled into the house.

"Look at this!" she cried. "I found these glasses under the porch window. They don't belong to us. Somebody must have been looking in and dropped them. Somebody has been spying on our house!"

"The man at the newspaper office!" Joe exclaimed.

"Let's see 'em," Frank asked.

A piece had been broken out of the left side of the frame!

"Our man, all right, Joe," he said. "We *were* followed, sure enough. Aunt Gertrude, which window was he looking in?"

She led the way to the far window on the porch which opened into the living room. Both boys began an examination of the spot. Finding no visible clues, Joe went for a magnifying glass. With it he spotted fresh fingerprints on the window sill.

"We'd better photograph these pronto," he said, and went to his father's basement laboratory for the equipment.

Mr. Hardy had taught his sons the latest method of using the necessary powder, camera, and developers. In a few minutes the fingerprints of the mysterious stranger were recorded. The brothers raced to Chief Collig with them. They told the chief of their adventure of the evening before.

The result was disappointing. The fingerprints did not belong to any wanted well-known criminal, nor to any local person with a police record.

"I'll send these prints along to the bureau in Washington if you want me to," Collig offered.

"No, thanks," said Frank. "We'll wait till Dad comes home."

Upon reaching home, the boys looked for matching fingerprints on the frames of the glasses, but as they had suspected, Aunt Gertrude's handling of them made this impossible. The glasses were placed on a shelf in the laboratory marked *visible evidence*.

Returning upstairs, the brothers were met by their mother. "Do you suppose that Peeping Tom will come again?" she asked anxiously. "Oh, dear, I wish your father were home!"

"Don't worry, Mother," Frank said quickly. "I think the fellow wanted to find out if we had the money at home. He probably overheard us talking and learned it's at the police station."

Twice that afternoon Frank and Joe dropped into the *News* office for more mail. In all, they were handed four letters. None had any bearing on their case. Each one named a smaller sum of money and obviously referred to some other loss.

"Well, we haven't found the owner of the two thousand yet," Frank said. "Now I'm convinced."

"Of what? That shooting-star brain of yours is likely to hit on anything. Well, shoot!"

"Just for that I shouldn't tell you, but here goes. I'm convinced the money really was stolen. That's why the person who lost it can't come out in the open and claim it."

"I'll bet you're right, Frank," his brother said. "So we can expect more trouble."

"Exactly."

The brothers agreed not to mention their worry to Mrs. Hardy or Aunt Gertrude. There was no need of frightening them. During a leisurely supper hour they discussed various other matters, including the night ball game they planned to attend, also the trip to North Woods.

"How is Callie?" Mrs. Hardy asked, smiling at Frank, who was taking the girl to the game. Her son thought Callie Shaw the nicest girl at Bayport High.

"All right, I guess," he answered. "I haven't talked to her since yesterday."

"Tsk, tsk!" Joe spoke up. "Such neglect!"

"Cut it," Frank begged. "And you'd better get busy soon, Joe, or Iola will go with someone else."

Joe glanced at the clock. He barely had time to drive out to the Morton farm to pick up Chet's sister Iola. Excusing himself, he left the table.

"See you at the ball park in three-quarters of an hour, Frank," he called.

Frank set off on foot thirty minutes later. Callie's house was only a few blocks from the Hardy home and was on the way to the ball field. The sun had set, and a cool evening breeze stirred the leaves of the big trees which shaded the avenue as he walked along.

The boy was deep in thought about the mystery on which he and Joe had stumbled. When would they hear again from the letter writer who signed himself Rainy Night?

Reaching a wooded area where the houses were far apart, he heard a slight rustle behind a hedge. Almost immediately a dark figure came hurtling over the evergreen hedge. Before Frank could dodge, the stranger had flung himself upon him in a diving tackle.

Frank was blindfolded and gagged before he could attempt to defend himself or cry out. His head was still spinning when he became aware of another man on the scene.

"You got him, eh? Good!"

"What now?" asked the second man.

"Into the car."

Four hands dragged Frank along the ground and heaved him onto the floor in the rear of a sedan!

CHAPTER V

The Ransom Demand

JOE HARDY, meanwhile, drove happily along the highway toward the Morton farm. The prospect of seeing what promised to be a good ball game pleased him, especially since he was to see it with Iola. Not only did Joe prefer being with her to any other girl, but she understood the finer points of baseball.

It was not long before Joe drew up to the Morton home. He slowed down, pulled off the highway into the driveway that led to the big house, and hopped out. Chet waved a greeting from the porch.

"Iola will be down in a minute," he said. "Hey, do you think the Bayport Bears'll win tonight?"

"Depends on their pitching," Joe replied, as he slid into a wicker chair beside his friend. "The Oakmont Blues are strong on the mound, you know. They don't give away any runs."

"Where you going to sit?" Chet asked.

"Behind first base. Aren't you coming along?"

"I'll drop down later."

"Why don't you come with Iola and me?"

Chet's reply was a big grin and a wink that seemed to rearrange the pattern of freckles on his pug nose. He would not be a third party.

"Here comes Iola now," he said.

The screen door opened and his sister stepped out. Iola was as slim as her brother was chubby, but she had the same kind of tilted nose and twinkling eyes. Shoulder-length black hair, parted in the middle, fell in soft waves. Both boys rose.

"Hello, Joe," she said.

"Ready for some grand-slam homers?" he asked.

"I'll settle for a couple of triple plays," Iola replied, dimpling.

"Let's go," Joe said. "We'll save you a seat, Chet. Frank's taking Callie. And how about a soda after the game?"

Soon the coupé was on its way back to Bayport. Joe and Iola became engrossed in discussing the forthcoming contest. She was afraid the Oakmont Blues were going to win.

Before the couple realized it, they were on the outskirts of the ball field. Joe parked the car, bought two tickets, and found seats behind the initial sack.

"I thought Frank and Callie would be here by

this time," Joe said, looking around at the rapidly filling stands. "We'll hold three seats as long as we can."

The Oakmont Blues trotted onto the field for their warm up. After they had batted a few times and chased a few fungoes, the Bayport Bears replaced them on the diamond.

Joe stood up now and again to gaze at the gathering crowd. Frank and Callie were nowhere in sight.

"I don't like this," Joe said, beginning to feel uneasy. "They should have been here twenty minutes ago."

Iola touched his arm. "Don't worry," she said. "Maybe they wanted to sit by themselves."

Joe knew Frank would not do this without telling him. He kept surveying the sea of faces of the newcomers. Finally he spotted Chet and waved him over to where they were sitting.

"Hiya, kids!" Chet bubbled. "Glad you saved a seat for me. Say, where are the others?"

"Frank and Callie haven't arrived," Joe said. He tried not to appear anxious, but the strange happenings of the past two days made him apprehensive about his brother.

Chet tossed a dime at a vendor and got a bag of peanuts by the return pitch. He offered his sister and Joe some and then settled back to enjoy the game.

Joe hardly noticed the Blues come to bat in the first inning. Despite a flurry of hits, he could not keep his mind on the game. Chet began to bounce around in his seat when a Bayport player belted a home run in the second, scoring two men ahead of him. The local team was ahead, 3 to 2.

"How do you like that?" Chet shouted.

"Swell." But Joe's increasing alarm outweighed his enthusiasm.

"I'm going to phone and see if I can find out what happened to Frank and Callie," he said, getting up. "Iola, will you wait here with Chet until I come back?"

"All right. Hope you locate 'em soon," she said cheerfully.

Joe hurried to a public telephone booth at the rear of the ball park. Quickly he dialed the Shaw home. Callie answered.

"Hello, Frank?"

"No. This is Joe."

"Where's Frank?"

"Hasn't he been there?"

"No, Joe. And I haven't heard from him. Has something happened?"

"I hope not," Joe replied tersely. "Callie, I

can't understand this. Will you stay where you are until you hear from me again?"

The little gasp on the other end of the line told Joe that Callie's concern over Frank was as deep as his own. She had heard about the mysterious two thousand dollars the boys had found, and also how they had located Chet's stolen truck minus its contents.

"Oh, Joe," she said, "I hope none of those awful men—"

"I'll let you know as soon as I find out anything," Joe promised.

He hung up and then quickly telephoned his home. Aunt Gertrude said Frank had left the house thirty minutes after Joe had.

Joe went for the boys' coupé and drove to Callie's house. From there he walked over the route, now dark, which he thought Frank would have taken, but reached home without finding his brother. Had he been trailing someone and not returned yet? Joe did not think so.

"I'll get a flashlight and look again," Joe told himself, as he unlocked the door. He wanted to examine the route to the ball field more carefully, especially the wooded section, in case Frank might have been attacked and was lying unconscious somewhere out of sight from the street.

Mrs. Hardy and Aunt Gertrude were startled to

see Joe. He wished he might be able to keep his fears from them, but they soon got the truth out of the worried boy.

"We'll all look," said Mrs. Hardy.

"I knew something terrible would come of your trying to find the owner of that bad money," Aunt Gertrude cried. "Where's my brother's stick? I'm going to take it along." She grabbed a hickory cane from the hall closet. "I'll beat the daylights out of anyone who has laid a hand on Frank!" she vowed.

"Good old Aunt Gertrude," Joe thought, as he raced upstairs for his flashlight.

The three hurried from the house and walked slowly along the street that led to Callie's. Joe led the way, flashing the light from side to side. When they reached the wood spot where Frank had been attacked, Joe bent down. Signs of a struggle were apparent to his trained eyes. Was it his brother who had been in a scuffle and who had dug his heels deep into the earth to resist being dragged off?

"Did you find something?" Mrs. Hardy called, hurrying to his side.

Her son pointed. Then something else he saw a few feet farther away sent a spasm of fear to the pit of his stomach.

There lay Frank's initialed handkerchief!

Joe had seen his brother arrange it neatly in his

breast pocket as they had finished dressing. Mrs. Hardy and Aunt Gertrude saw the handkerchief, too. There was no doubt now. Somebody had ambushed Frank. Had he been carried off? And where to?

Two lines that looked as though they had been made by shoe heels led to the curb. There were no further signs of a possible kidnaping, but the flashlight showed oil stains in the street as if a car had stood in the lonely spot for some time before being driven off.

Mrs. Hardy began to tremble. "Oh, my boy, my boy!" she said. "How can we find him?"

Aunt Gertrude kept her emotions under firm control. "Come," she said. "We'll go back home and get the police busy at once. Joe, you run ahead and phone them. I'll take care of your mother."

The boy reached the Hardy house just as a tall, distinguished-looking man was striding up the front walk. In one hand he carried a traveling bag, in the other a bulging briefcase.

"Dad!"

Mr. Hardy turned to greet his son. His keen dark eyes caught the look of alarm in Joe's face.

"Dad, we're afraid Frank's been attacked! Carried off!"

"Easy, son. Come inside and let me get this thing straight."

In their living room, Joe was just breathlessly beginning his story of the recent mysterious happenings when his mother and aunt came hurrying into the room. Greetings were brief and Mrs. Hardy became calmer now that her husband was home. Joe continued his story. The detective paced the floor as he listened, while Mrs. Hardy and Aunt Gertrude sat by, their faces reflecting their anxiety.

As Joe finished, there was a rap on the door. In rushed Chet and Iola.

"Where's Frank?" Iola cried. "I just couldn't watch the game any longer. We phoned Callie. I . . ."

The telephone rang. Mr. Hardy picked it up. "Hello. Fenton Hardy speaking."

"This is Rainy Night. We have your son, Hardy," a man's steely voice came over the wire. "Send us two one-thousand-dollar bills if you want him back alive."

Though alarmed, the detective's jaw tensed with anger. His voice had the edge of a cold blade as he answered. "Whoever you are, I want to remind you that there's a law against kidnaping."

"You're telling me!" came the cool reply. "But you dicks ain't catching us."

"Release that boy immediately," Mr. Hardy said, as everybody in the room stood electrified.

"Not till you pay!"

Mr. Hardy, though exasperated, was worried. His bluff had not worked. "How shall we pay you the money?" he asked.

"You'll know in the morning. Have the cash ready by eight thirty." The receiver clicked in the detective's ear.

Immediately Mr. Hardy put in a call to Central and asked that the recent call be traced. Then he told his wife and son that the man on the wire had demanded a ransom for the delivery of Frank.

"Don't any of you say a word about this until I give the word," Mr. Hardy warned. "It may mean Frank's life if we're not careful."

In trembling anxiety Chet and Iola went home, pledged to keep the secret. Then Joe telephoned to Callie, telling her not to worry, and saying he would pick up his car in the morning.

Sleep came fitfully to all in the Hardy household. In the morning they showed the strain of a night of anguish.

While they were listlessly eating breakfast, the doorbell rang. It was exactly eight o'clock. Joe rushed to answer. An expressman stood on the porch, holding a cage partially wrapped in burlap and containing two pigeons.

"Who sent these?" Joe asked in surprise.

"Dunno. All I do is deliver stuff I'm given."

Joe signed for the birds and carried the cage into the living room. The other Hardys rushed from the dining room.

"What in creation!" Aunt Gertrude exclaimed.

Mrs. Hardy looked at her husband for an explanation. "So this is the way we're to send the ransom money," the detective said.

Joe looked at the pigeons' legs. "There're not banded," he remarked. "Homing pigeons are usually numbered, aren't they, Dad?"

"Yes. A very clever person is behind this move," Mr. Hardy said grimly. "These pigeons will fly straight to the culprits who kidnaped Frank, and we'll never find out who they are. But," the detective added with set jaw, "I'll find a way to trap them!"

"Please don't, Fenton," Mrs. Hardy cried. "Send the money and get Frank back!"

Aunt Gertrude spluttered and daubed her eyes. "You'd better do it, Fenton," she said.

CHAPTER VI

Tailing a Pigeon

CONSCIOUSNESS rushed back into Frank's brain. He was aware of a distant church bell tolling eight o'clock. Was it morning or evening? He could see nothing because of the blindfold fastened tightly around his head.

The boy's ankles were tied, his wrists bound behind him, and the gag still was in his mouth. Now the whole picture came back to him. After he had been attacked and thrown into the car, a gruff voice had said:

"Easy now. This kid's worth two grand."

There had followed a ride of considerable distance. The car had stopped and the boy had been aware of being carried into a house.

The last words he had heard were, "Let him have a good jab to hold him over!" A needle had punctured the skin on Frank's arm. Then he had blacked out.

How long he had lain in the darkness the boy did not know. His whole body ached from the tight cords with which his wrists and ankles were bound. What day was it, he wondered.

With every ounce of effort, Frank rolled over and over on an earthen floor until he hit a wall. Rubbing his head against it, he was able to slip off the blindfold. By the daylight coming through a dirty window high above him, Frank realized he was in a cellar.

On the floor near him lay a piece of broken pipe. Frank wriggled across the dirty cellar floor. After a great deal of painful maneuvering he was able to bring his wrist bonds in contact with the jagged edge of the broken drainpipe. The pipe rolled away, and the boy had to wedge it between the floor and the wall before he could saw the rope back and forth across the rusty edge of the pipe. The effort was painful and exhausting. But at last the rope parted and his hands were free. Quickly he loosened his gag and untied the rope that bound his ankles. He rose and walked around to stretch his cramped muscles.

The house was silent. Were the thugs upstairs, ready to deal with him further?

There was no door leading to the outside, so Frank noiselessly lifted the window, fastening it with a rusty hook. He sprang upward, at the same time thrusting his head out of the window and catching his weight on his elbows. Nobody was in sight.

Digging his toes against the side of the cellar wall, Frank cautiously wormed his way through the low window. In the morning light he could see weather-beaten shutters, some open, some shut, hanging grotesquely from what obviously was a farmhouse, and the front door stood open on a broken hinge. The place seemed deserted.

Frank looked around and tried to get his bearings. To the north was a wooded mountain with a dip in the peak. Recognizing the mountaintop formation, he decided that the farm must be located on the same road on which they had found Chet's abandoned truck—only farther from town.

"Those birds must know this territory well," he thought.

Remembering another farmhouse a mile or so in the direction of Black Horse Pike, Frank set off through the field. He was faint from hunger and the drug, but he kept on. It must still be early morning, he figured. As he plodded up the lane to the house, the farmer's wife saw him coming and opened the door. She surveyed the disheveled boy skeptically.

"May I use your telephone?" he asked. "I'm Frank Hardy, and I want to call my home in Bay-port."

"Hardy?" she repeated.

"My father's Fenton Hardy, the detective."

"You on a case of his?" she asked, having read in the newspapers from time to time about Mr. Hardy and his sons. "Or just lost in the woods overnight?"

"Neither one." Frank smiled. "But it is important that I get in touch with my father."

He put his call through. As he waited, the boy noticed that the hands on a mantel clock stood at eight twenty-five.

Mr. Hardy answered. "Frank? Is this you, Frank? Hold the wire a second." His voice boomed into the distance, "Don't let that pigeon go!"

Frank was perplexed. He could hear sounds of the detective returning to the telephone.

"We were just going to get the doctor for your mother," Mr. Hardy said.

Frank was not alarmed by the words. He recognized them as a Hardy code. Translated, they meant:

"If you are being held and are allowed to say only what you're told to, sneeze or cough twice. If not, give the word that all is well."

"The weather is fine," Frank replied, and he heard his father breathe a sigh of relief. "Dad," he continued, "will you pick me up on Black Horse

Pike? I'll walk there. I'm calling from a farm on the North Woods road."

Joe was listening, too. "We'll burn up the tires!" he shouted.

Frank hung up, thanked the woman, and paid her for the call. She insisted that he sit down in the kitchen and have some rolls and milk, which he accepted gratefully. His feeling of weakness and dizziness was rapidly disappearing.

"Is that old farmhouse down the road deserted?" he asked, pointing in the direction of the building, barely visible over the trees, where he had spent the night.

"Yes, 'tis," she replied. "The old folks passed away and nobody wants the place. Land's worked out, but John, my husband, and I always say 'twas their own fault. They didn't rotate their crops like the county agent told 'em to."

"Anybody been using it since they left?" Frank asked casually.

The woman laughed. "That tumble-down place? Who'd want to stay there?"

"Tramps might—or somebody looking for a hide-out."

The farm woman bristled. "Young man, we don't tolerate no folks like that in this peace-abiding neighborhood!"

Frank could have pointed out the error in her

contention, but he said nothing. Thanking her for her hospitality, he departed. He walked to the intersection of the Black Horse Pike, where he sat down and waited to be picked up.

When Mr. Hardy and Joe arrived in the detective's car, there was an enthusiastic exchange of greetings, then a quick ride back to the Hardy home. On the way, Frank was told about the ransom demand that had come over the telephone the evening before and of the crate of pigeons that had arrived that morning.

"I was just going to release one of the pigeons when you phoned," Mr. Hardy said.

The boys' mother and Aunt Gertrude were overjoyed to see Frank safely home once more. They listened spellbound as he related all that had happened to him since he had left the house to pick up Callie at her home.

"I wonder why they left you unguarded?" Joe asked.

"They probably thought the hypo would make me sleep longer than it did."

"Those men may return again," Mr. Hardy reasoned. "We'll notify the police to post a guard at the old farmhouse." He reached for the telephone.

"And a guard for this house, too," Aunt Gertrude demanded. "Those cutthroats will stop at nothing."

"Good idea." The detective notified the police, who promised to send out a detail immediately to the Hardy home, and to notify the state police to take care of the abandoned farm.

It was midday when he received a return call from the police saying that the deserted house had been watched constantly but that nobody had come there yet.

"Dad," said Frank, "what would you think of our releasing one of the pigeons and following it to the crooks' hide-out?"

"You must have been reading by mind, son. Call the airport and charter a plane, Joe. Then get our binoculars."

Joe quickly made arrangements to hire a four-place plane, while Frank ate a substantial meal. Then the detective and his sons set off for the flying field with one of the pigeons in the cage.

They were greeted at the Ace Air Service by a level-eyed young pilot named Jack Wayne.

"Where would you like me to take you?" he asked genially.

"That depends upon this pigeon," Mr. Hardy answered, and quickly explained their plan.

"I've chased the enemy many a time." The pilot laughed. "But this is my first time chasing a bird!"

The four climbed into the plane. It taxied down

the runway and, gathering speed, rose easily into the air.

"We'll let the pigeon out at a thousand feet," Mr. Hardy said.

When they reached that altitude, Joe released the bird. It flew away from the plane and began circling to orient itself.

The pilot kept right behind the bird, flying round and round in ever-widening circles. Suddenly the bird zoomed up, then shot downward, probably frightened by the plane. Wayne treated the Hardys to a chute-the-chutes maneuver to keep the pigeon in front of him.

"Take it easy," Mr. Hardy cautioned.

Joe kept his binoculars trained on the pigeon. Finally the bird got its beam and flew straight toward the south.

"That pigeon really can travel!" the pilot exclaimed admiringly.

After half an hour of steady flying toward the south, the pilot turned to Mr. Hardy. "How far do you want to follow it, sir?"

"Until your fuel's low."

The detective and his sons conferred on the situation. There was no telling how far the pigeon would fly. The fuel supply of the plane might be exhausted long before the bird alighted.

"One thing is certain," Frank said. "The pigeon

wouldn't have carried the money anywhere near Bayport."

"Which proves," Joe added, "that the thugs who kidnaped you have pals in some other part of the country."

Ten minutes later the pilot said he would look for a place to land his ship. The fuel supply was low. Disappointed, the Hardys gave up the chase.

"Maybe we can trace the sender of the pigeons through the express company," Frank suggested as the plane was refueled at a small country airport.

"I've already done that," his father said. "The sender gave a phony home address outside Bayport."

After they had returned to Bayport and paid the flier, the Hardys got into their car and drove home, disappointed that their mission had brought no result.

"Dad, what is this new case you are working on in Washington?" Joe asked presently. "Can you let us in on it?"

Mr. Hardy looked searchingly at his sons. "It's a top-secret assignment," he said, "but I know I can trust you to keep it."

With rapt attention, Frank and Joe listened while the famous detective unfolded a tale of foreign intrigue. United States currency was being stolen in various South American countries and the Caribbean. It was suspected the money was being used to carry out some nefarious schemes. What these were had not yet been discovered.

"I'm working with the FBI on the United States end of the case," Mr. Hardy said. "Other detectives are operating in the foreign countries."

"Sure sounds exciting," Joe commented. "You have no idea what the thieves are using the money for?"

"Not yet. But we think it is being spent in the United States."

"Is the money being smuggled in across the border?" Frank asked.

"We don't know yet."

"It could be by boat or plane, then?"

"Yes."

Frank and Joe looked at each other. Had their find of two thousand dollars anything to do with their father's case?

CHAPTER VII

A Suspicious Salesman

"Dad, could it be possible we're working on the same case?" Joe asked him.

"I'll know better when I see the bills you found. I have the serial numbers of some of the stolen money."

"The two thousand is at police headquarters," Frank said. "Let's go there now."

His father agreed. Maybe the day's work would prove to have some value after all.

Frank drove the car and stopped at Bayport's police headquarters. The Hardys went in.

"I'm glad you got away from those thugs," Chief Collig said to Frank.

"So am I." The youth grinned, then sobered. "Any news of Chet Morton's stolen stuff?"

The chief said he was sorry to report that there was not a trace of it so far. "But I'm certain it's not in Bayport," he added quickly.

Frank and Joe were not so sure.

"If the loot's out in the country, the state police will probably land it soon," Collig assured them.

"I hope so," said Frank, and added that he and Joe would like to show the mysterious money to their father.

Collig opened the safe and took out the wallet, which he placed on a table. Mr. Hardy withdrew the bills one by one and very slowly began to count them aloud. Frank noticed his father's eyes scanning every detail of the printing as he flipped the money over.

"Well, that's two thousand, all right," the detective remarked as he finished. He handed it back to the chief.

"I could have told you that," Collig said with a frown. He had expected more than this from the great detective.

Mr. Hardy thanked the officer for his trouble. He and his sons returned to their car.

"Find out anything?" Joe asked eagerly.

"Yes. One of those hundred-dollar bills had a serial number we're looking for!"

"Then our cases are related!" Frank cried excitedly.

"Apparently. We three are in this together," Mr. Hardy said with a smile of satisfaction.

"Couldn't be better!" Joe shouted enthusiastically. "Look out, Rainy Night, here come the Hardys!"

Arriving home, they found Aunt Gertrude reading the evening *News* on the front porch.

"Look at this!" she cried out, waving the newspaper in front of them. " 'Hardy boy captured, released by thugs.' Why do newspapers get everything mixed up? Frank got away by himself! I'll write to that editor!"

The boys were amused as well as pleased at their aunt's loyalty. Even though she objected to their working on mystery cases, she was always secretly proud of their exploits and wanted no one else to be given any credit for their achievements.

The story went on to say that Frank was safe and that the authorities were looking for the kidnapers. As she read on, Aunt Gertrude grew even more excited.

"I can just imagine what those wretched criminals are figuring now," she sputtered. "They'll probably try to come right back here and take Frank away again!"

"With the police guarding us?" her nephew asked.

"Just the same," Mrs. Hardy spoke up, "I'd feel better if those awful men didn't know where Frank and Joe are."

"You have a good point," her husband agreed.

"Boys, why not go on that long camping trip you were talking about?"

His sons grinned. "We planned to go to North Woods this week end and hunt for Chet's stolen stuff."

"Excellent idea," his father said. "Combine work with pleasure."

"North Woods," Aunt Gertrude snorted, "is full of wild dogs. You boys must be out of your minds."

"The stories about the dogs are only rumors," Frank reminded her.

Mr. Hardy suggested it was possible someone had started the rumor to keep intruders away from the place. He warned his sons to be on guard.

The boys' mother announced a new worry. Her sons might be followed into the wilderness by the kidnapers.

"Why not try leaving here without letting anyone see you?" she suggested. "Stay at Chet's house tonight and start from there in the early morning."

Frank and Joe liked their mother's plan. They telephoned Chet, and also Biff Hooper and Tony Prito. The latter two promised to meet them at the Morton farm right after breakfast.

"Chet sure sounded as low as a sunken submarine," Frank commented. "I guess his dad and uncle were pretty sore when they heard what happened."

"Iola told me he's got to work on the farm all summer long to pay for the stuff if it's not found," Joe said.

Frank chuckled. "That'll take off the pounds. Bayport High won't recognize its first-squad center."

Frank and Joe packed their equipment in the trunk compartment of Mr. Hardy's car. After dark they got in and lay on the floor of the rear seat, while their father drove to the Mortons'. The boys did not show their heads until they were at the farm.

"If anybody is looking for us, they won't know whether we've left the house or not," Joe remarked.

They unloaded the gear and the detective turned the car around. Wishing his sons good luck, he said he was going to Washington for further checking on the stolen-currency case.

Frank and Joe picked up their heavy packs and entered the house. To their surprise they found that Callie was visiting Iola, and the girls had prepared a farewell snack for them and Chet.

"Iola made a cake as high as North Woods Mountain," Callie said laughingly, as they all sat down.

"Better eat as much of it as you can, Chet," Joe advised, " 'cause you'll need a lot of energy fighting those wild dogs."

Chet's eyes popped. "I thought you said that was only a rumor. Listen, fellows, if it's true, I'm not—"

"You're not what?" Joe persisted. "Not going

to have another trip in your life till you pay for those stolen rifles and—"

The fun went on until bedtime. After a hearty breakfast the next morning the young people went out on the porch to wait for Biff and Tony. They had been sitting there only a few minutes when they saw a man, carrying a bulging bag, coming up the driveway. He was fairly tall, had light-colored hair, and shrewd-looking eyes.

"Do you want to see my father?" Chet asked him.

"Anybody'll do," the stranger replied. "I'm selling insect repellent. Most wonderful stuff in the world. Use it on the farm or anywhere. Kills flies, moths, mosquitoes."

Chet became interested. Mosquito repellent— the only thing he had forgotten for the camping trip.

"We could use some of that," he said. "Just what we fellows need for our camping trip."

The man smiled. "Camping trip, eh? Then you'll want a lot of my repellent. Plenty of flies in the woods. Where you going?"

"To North . . ."

Joe's elbow jabbed into his friend's ribs. Chet was telling the stranger too much!

"North—uh—uh—North Carolina. That is, some day," Chet went on, embarrassed.

"How much repellent you want?" the salesman asked.

"None, I guess," Chet replied glumly, realizing he had made a blunder.

"As you please," the other said without resorting to any further high-pressure sales talk.

He picked up his bag and walked down the drive. As he shuffled off toward the next farmhouse, Joe grasped Frank's arm.

"I don't like this," he said. "If that man were a real salesman, he wouldn't have let us off so easy."

"You're right. And he's blond and tall. So was that chap who followed me from the *News* office."

"I'll bet he came here to spy," Joe declared. "I'd sure like to find out. Say, will you girls help us out?"

"How?" they asked. Both girls had done sleuthing for the boys before.

"Follow that man. Use the fields, so he can't see you. Check if he really is a salesman. Telephone when you want Chet to pick you up in the car."

Callie and Iola set off on a run along the path that led to the nearest neighbor. Half an hour later the farm telephone rang. Joe jumped to answer it.

"You guessed right," Iola told him. "That man was no salesman. He didn't stop at a single house. After we followed him nearly a mile, keeping out of his sight, he suddenly hopped in a car parked at the side of the road and went off."

"Did you get the license number?"

"Sorry. No."

Chet drove down, picked up the girls, and was soon back. Meanwhile the Hardys discussed the case.

"We've proved one thing," Frank said. "That man was sent here to learn something. We'll have to be mighty careful on our trip. I'm only sorry Chet practically told him where we are going."

In a few minutes Biff Hooper and Tony Prito arrived in a car with Tony's mother.

"Hiya!" Biff shouted as he saw the Hardys. "Where's Chet? Eating another stack of flapjacks?"

"Believe it or not, he's on the job!" Frank laughed. "Giving the jalopy a last inspection."

Tony and Biff were told the latest developments in the mystery and the recent episode of the pseudo salesman.

"I've a hunch we'll see him again," Joe said. "He may even follow us to North Woods."

"We'll be ready for him," Tony vowed.

After piling their camping equipment in Chet's car, the boys climbed in. The jalopy snorted and started off down the road.

"Let's park at that farmhouse where I made the telephone call," Frank said. "Then we can start the hike to the woods from there."

This agreed upon, Chet turned off into the lonely

road. When they arrived at the farmhouse, the woman gladly let them leave the car behind the barn. The boys took out their gear and after a cold drink of water at the pump started their trek toward North Woods.

As they passed the deserted house where Frank had been held, the boy's spine tingled. Had the thugs planned to leave him there to die, he wondered? Or would they have freed him after the ransom had been collected?

The campers walked another mile, then headed into the woods at the point where they thought Chet's stolen stuff might have been carried in. Upon reaching the brook where the suspect's footprints had ended, they stopped to confer on which way to proceed. The trees and underbrush stretched for miles, wild and apparently uninhabited.

"Well, you detectives," Tony said, "where in this jungle did that thief go?"

Frank was sure they would have taken the path of least resistance into the forest. After all, the canoe would be an unwieldy thing to carry in dense woodland.

"Okay," Tony said with a grin. "You find it."

The boys resumed the trek, with Frank and Joe in the lead. After they had pressed forward for an hour, Chet stopped and flung his pack to the ground. "Say, fellows, do you know where you're going?" he puffed.

"Sure," said Frank. "In the direction the crooks took."

"How do you know?"

"By this." Frank had just spied what might be a clue.

He bent down beside a rough rock, twice the size of a man's head. Somebody apparently had stepped on it and slipped, making a deep heel impression in the moss beside it.

Frank whipped a magnifying glass from his pack and examined the rock. It revealed minute shreds of leather where the uneven surface of the boulder had abraded the shoe.

"I think we're on the right track," he said as he sheathed his glass. "Come on, Chet."

An hour later the boys stopped for lunch. Then after a good rest they moved on again, following a mountain stream. They kept their eyes alert for the rest of the afternoon, but were not rewarded by any further evidence that the thieves had preceded them. More than once the Hardys had to reassure their friends that they were on the right track. It was the only halfway open route by which heavily laden men could have penetrated the densely forested area.

Finally they decided to make camp. Tony prepared a satisfying hot meal of beans and bacon.

As the boys ate it, Chet gave a volcanic sigh. "I'm afraid that stolen stuff's gone forever," he said. "Listen, fellows, you haven't any plans for the summer. How about giving me a hand at the farm to help pay for the stuff?"

"Never milked a cow in my life," Tony used as an excuse.

"Pitching hay makes me sneeze something awful," said Biff. He shifted his long legs and yawned.

"Doctor says bouncing on a tractor is bad for my heart," Joe piped up.

Chet refused to laugh. "Then you simply got to find that stuff," he declared.

"We?" Frank chortled. "We're only helping you."

Chet grunted, took an extra helping of beans, and announced he was hitting the sack early. All the boys, tired from their long trek, crawled into their sleeping bags within half an hour after eating.

In the middle of the night they awoke suddenly. Some sound had aroused the campers. They listened. In the distance an animal howled.

But there had been another kind of sound, too, the boys were sure. Yes, there it was again.

A wailing siren!

CHAPTER VIII

The Night Prowler

THE campers sat bolt upright as the siren wailed again, its mournful tone dying out like a fading echo in the distance.

"That's the same sound we heard over the ocean, Joe!" Frank said in a hoarse whisper. "Do you think it could be the same siren?"

"What would it be doing 'way out here?"

Instinctively both boys had looked up, associating the sound with a plane. But there was no drone of an aircraft overhead.

"Hey, what's up?" Chet called. "Wha-what was that? Let's get out of here!"

"Where to?" Tony asked. "The treetops?"

Chet subsided. The boys listened, but the mysterious wailing sound was not repeated.

"You're sure it was the same sound you heard just before you found the money?" Biff asked the Hardys.

"It sure was," Joe declared.

This gave Chet an idea. "Say, fellows," he said, grinning, "if any more money drops out of the sky, it's mine to pay for the stolen stuff!"

"Try and get it with me here," said Tony.

Propped up on their elbows, the five boys conjectured about the source of the noise and what might happen next. Suddenly the howling of the animal they had heard a few minutes before began again. It seemed to be nearer now.

"It's a wild dog!" Chet cried out. "He's smelled us. He might bring his whole pack here!"

Biff suggested building a fire to frighten off the animal.

"But that'll focus attention on us," Frank objected. "If the siren had anything to do with the money Joe and I found, my kidnapers might spot us."

The others agreed and waited in the dark. Presently the howling animal became quiet, so the boys settled themselves once more in their sleeping bags.

"I have nothing to worry about anyway," Biff called. "Chet's the best eating for a wild dog."

All but Chet smiled drowsily and went to sleep. During the rest of the night the woods were quiet, except for lulling noises of insects. Chet was the last to awaken next morning, and only then because Biff dumped him out of his sleeping bag.

"Good night, can't you let a fellow rest?" Chet objected. Then a second later he caught the savory aroma of bacon, frying crisply in the skillet which Joe held over a campfire. "Nothing like bacon and eggs in the forest," he beamed, and crawled out.

While the boys were enjoying breakfast, they tried to figure out the disturbance of the previous night.

"You know how sounds carry," Biff said. "The wind was pretty strong last night from the south. That siren might have carried here from a town's firehouse."

"Yeah," Chet said. He spread another slice of bread and jam. "Things don't seem so spooky in the daytime, do they?"

"It's my guess the siren was much closer than that," Frank insisted. "Not more than two miles away."

"Say, it's eight o'clock," Biff said, after glancing at his watch. "Think I'll listen to the news. We might learn something that will explain that wailing siren."

"How you going to listen to the news?" Chet asked. "We haven't any radio."

"Oh, yes, we have," Biff replied with a sly grin. He reached into his pack and drew out a radio no larger than the palm of his hand.

"Swell gadget," Joe said in admiration.

Biff dialed the Bayport station. The voice of the

announcer was excited, telling of the disappearance of a plane. The pilot, Jack Wayne, had taken off from Bayport the evening before. A short time later he had contacted the airfield by radio.

"I'm in trouble!" he had cried. "Pirates!" Nothing more had been heard from him.

"It's thought he may have crashed on the ocean or in the woodlands beyond Bayport," the announcer said. "The Coast Guard has been alerted, and State Police have started a search."

The Hardys looked at each other, dismayed. Jack Wayne! The pilot who had taken them up only two days before!

"If Wayne came down in these woods," said Frank soberly, "I'm afraid he's in bad shape."

The campers decided to combine looking for him with hunting for the articles stolen from the Morton truck. They listened to the rest of the broadcast while packing up, but there was no other news of particular interest to the boys.

Frank and Joe suggested that they should go straight through the woods in the direction from which the siren sound had come, and the five set off. As they scrambled along through the dense thickets, Chet talked continuously about the disturbing broadcast. What would a pirate be doing in the air? How could somebody capture a person in flight?

"A stowaway might have knocked Wayne out," Frank suggested. "But you've given me an idea, Chet. Maybe Wayne didn't crash. He may have been kidnaped!"

Nevertheless, all the boys watched for signs of an accident, as they pressed deeper into the pathless woodland. Progress was necessarily slow because of the rough terrain and their heavy packs.

Chet grunted and puffed, complaining intermittently. "We're on a wild-goose chase," he grumbled. "How could anyone carrying a canoe go through country like this?"

"Would you rather be sweating it out on a hayfield to pay for the stolen stuff?" Biff reminded him.

Chet said no more until he reached the edge of a little stream. "Hey, look here!" he shouted gleefully.

The boys ran to his side. Chet pointed to deep tracks at the water's edge.

"Maybe that wild animal we heard last night made 'em," he said.

"Deer don't howl," Tony scoffed.

"It was a heavy buck," Frank observed. "The prints are deep."

"You're all so smart," Chet scowled.

"Thank you!" The boys bowed in unison.

"Daniel Boone Detective Agency, Incorporated!" Joe added.

"Bah!" Chet grumbled.

Talk ceased as the party began ascending a rugged slope. The going was hard. It became necessary to pull on saplings to assist in the climb. Perspiration drenched the shirts of the hikers by the time they reached the ridge. Chet was puffing, and his face was as red as a beet.

"Let's rest here awhile, fellows, and look over the valley," he suggested.

"Maybe we can spot something from a tree," said Tony.

He walked toward an old fir, which towered like a sentinel. The wind had snapped off the ends of several limbs and they stuck out grotesquely like a ladder with one rail gone.

"Stand on my shoulders and catch the first branch," Biff offered.

He leaned over to help him, and Tony soon was on his way up the tree. When he reached the top he shaded his eyes with one hand.

"Swell view," he called. "I can see all the way to the bay. Boy, could I use a swim in it right now!"

"Any sign of the plane?" Joe called up.

"Or of the thieves who stole my stuff?" Chet shouted.

The reply was negative to both questions, but Tony continued to gaze around him in every direction. Suddenly he cried out:

"I see something shiny way off there." He pointed deeper into the forest. "Maybe it's part of the lost plane."

The youth climbed down and led the way over swampy ground and through a tangle of tamaracks in the direction of the gleaming object. After an hour's hike, he said:

"I guess I've found it. It's not a plane. It's a pond."

The boys followed Tony through a clump of thick brush. Beyond it in the sun lay a good-sized body of water. Chet brightened at once.

"Oh, brother, I'll bet it's full of fish!" he exclaimed.

Throwing himself on the edge of the water, he opened his pack and took out a fishline and hook.

"Here's some bait," Biff offered, spotting a colorful caterpillar on a leaf.

Chet put it on the hook and flung the line into the pond. The caterpillar lay on the surface a moment, then a fish leaped for the bait.

"Wow!" Chet exclaimed. "He's a big one!"

The boy played out the line as best he could. Without a reel it was difficult. The fish raced back and forth, flashing to the surface three times before Chet landed it.

"A bass. And a whopper!" he cried. "Five pounds if it's an ounce. Now for a feast, fellows."

The other boys decided on a swim first. They stripped off their clothes. Chet complained that since he had caught the fish, his companions should clean it, but they paid no attention to him.

"Race you across the pond, Frank," Joe called, taking a shallow dive.

He beat his brother to the far side by only one length. They pulled up on the bank and sat down.

Frank, looking about him, noticed the remains of a campfire near by. He got up and walked over to it. There were several backbones of fish. Someone had cooked and eaten there recently!

"I wonder if it was one of the crew we're after," he said excitedly. "Say, here are some good footprints to follow."

The brothers tried to follow them, but the going was too painful on their bare feet.

"Let's come back later when we have shoes on," Joe suggested.

Swimming back to the other shore they reported their discovery.

"Now we're getting somewhere," said Chet, "but, gosh, I'm awful tired. Can't we wait awhile before we chase those guys?"

The Hardys offered to follow the trail of the footprints while the others did some fishing. Immediately after lunch Joe and Frank resumed their search for the unknown fisherman. His marks were plainly visible in the soft ground near the pond, but as soon as the earth grew hard, the trail ended.

"Let's continue in the same direction," Frank suggested. "The fellow may have a cabin up ahead."

They went on for a quarter of a mile but found nothing, and decided that he must have changed his course. Frank thought it might be a good idea for all of the campers to remain in the vicinity of the pond for a while.

"That man will probably come back," he said.

The brothers rejoined their friends. At sunset they moved camp across the pond just out of sight of the stranger's old campfire.

The boys enjoyed Tony's catch of sunfish, then listened to the radio. There was no word from the missing Jack Wayne, the newscaster said. Presently Chet began to yawn loudly, and all decided that it was time to turn in.

"Don't sleep too hard," Frank told his brother. "Keep one eye open for visitors."

Joe nodded. It was not long before the heavy breathing of the other three boys blended with the sounds of the woodland night. Frank and Joe dozed fitfully. An hour later Frank leaned over and nudged his brother.

"I'm sure I heard footsteps," he whispered, looking around. "There they are again!"

A slight sound of crackling underbrush came to their ears. Suddenly a light flashed. It was trained directly on the Hardy brothers.

"Who are you?" Frank shouted, leaping out of his bag and arousing the entire camp.

There was no answer. The light went out and retreating footsteps hurried off in the underbrush.

Frank put on his shoes, grabbed his flashlight, and darted after the intruder.

"Chet, Biff, Tony, watch camp! There may be others! Come on, Joe!" he shouted.

One thing was certain; the stranger knew his way in the dark. Presently he was so far ahead of the boys, that the sound of his sprinting footsteps died out completely.

"I hate to give up," Frank said in disgust. "But we'd never find him now."

The brothers turned back, wondering if the intruder had been one of the thieves they were after, or only some hermit who did not want his hide-out to be discovered.

Reaching camp, they found the others excited and worried. Biff had picked up a note the mysterious caller had dropped. It was evident that the purpose of his visit had been to leave a warning. The piece of dirty paper bore a message written in pencil:

Get out of these woods. You're in danger.

"Maybe we ought to leave," Chet said.

The Hardys felt that the warning note proved that a person or persons in North Woods for some very good reason did not want the boys around. Unless the writer had something to hide, why would he mind their presence?

"We'll stay," said Frank.

"Let's set up watches," Joe suggested.

Since it was already one o'clock, each was assigned to an hour's sentry duty. However, the rest of the night passed without incident.

At six they all arose. Frank, who had been on watch during the past hour, said he had discovered a small, clear stream that emptied into the pond.

"Good drinking water," he said.

Chet was sent off with the canteens, while the others prepared breakfast. He had been gone only a few minutes when he let out a war whoop.

"I'll bet a snake bit him!" Biff exclaimed.

The boys dashed in the direction from which Chet's shout had come. Chet was leaning far over an undercut in the bank, tugging at something which they could not see.

"What's the matter?" Frank asked.

The stout boy turned his head and motioned. "Come here quick! I've found the stolen canoe!"

CHAPTER IX

The Answering Whistle

In the tiny lagoon, almost hidden by the eelgrass at the water's edge, floated a canoe.

"Are you sure it's the same canoe, Chet?" Joe asked.

"Sure I'm sure." Chet ran his fingers along the underside of the gunwale, then smiled. "And here's something to prove it."

He pointed to a bad nick in the varnished wood, saying Wells Hardware had knocked something off the original price because of the imperfection.

"This is the best clue yet," Frank said enthusiastically. "Maybe the other stolen stuff isn't far away."

"You mean the thief hid the canoe here?" Chet asked.

"It might have drifted down the river," Joe suggested. "There aren't any paddles in it."

"Let's go up the river after breakfast and take a look," Frank said.

As the Hardys fashioned two crude paddles from a split tree limb, Chet put a small pack and three sandwiches in the canoe. Then while Biff and Tony remained to watch the camp in case the thief returned, the other three started up the river. Joe kneeled in the bow and Frank in the stern. Chet sat down in the middle facing Frank.

"Joe, you watch the left bank for signs of the thief," Frank suggested as his crude paddle bit into the shallow, rock-filled water. "I'll take the right."

"What about me?" Chet queried. "Don't I look anywhere?"

"You're ballast," Joe needled. "All you do is sit tight."

But Frank was more serious. "Watch the rear, Chet. See if anybody steps out of hiding after we go past."

Thus posted, the three boys proceeded slowly upstream. All eyes were strained for a glimpse of a human being, a hut, or any other place where the stolen rifles, tools, and camp equipment might be hidden.

For a long time there was silence except for the gurgling of the ripples around the rocks and the dipping of the paddles. Then Chet shouted:

"I saw a splash! Back there, where we passed that high bank."

Frank and Joe looked around, letting the canoe drift backward. Then the boys saw another splash. A playful animal was sliding down the muddy bank into the water.

"An otter!" Joe laughed.

Nevertheless, the Hardys praised Chet for his alertness and pushed ahead again. Fifteen minutes later Joe let out a whistle. He indicated a lean-to near the riverbank.

"Let's investigate it," he said, resting his paddle.

They landed and Chet held onto the canoe while Frank and Joe looked in the lean-to. A pair of hiking boots stood in one corner.

"They're new," Frank remarked as he examined them. "Say, here's a long scratch." The shiny leather on the right one had been deeply marred.

"Might have been the fellow who slipped on the rock in the woods," Joe guessed. "I wonder where he is."

Meanwhile, Chet was looking around uneasily. The note had warned them of danger. Since they had chosen to disregard the warning, someone might take a pot shot at the boys any minute.

"Listen, fellows," he said, "that guy's got the advantage over us. We'd better scram."

"Nothing doing," said Frank. "One of us ought

to hide here to see who comes for the shoes. Suppose
we all paddle off, so if he's around here now, he
won't be suspicious. One of us can sneak back
through the woods."

Joe volunteered. At a bend in the river he
hopped ashore and carefully retraced his way to the
lean-to.

Five, ten, fifteen minutes went by. Merely sitting and waiting behind a large tree began to irk the
restless boy. He decided to do a little scouting.

"But which way?" he wondered.

While Joe stood trying to decide, his nostrils
caught the scent of wood smoke. He knew he was
too far from the boys' camp for smoke to be detected
at this distance. Someone in the vicinity had a fire!
Turning slowly and sniffing the air at intervals, he
finally concluded it was coming from a direction at
right angles to the river.

Keeping an alert watch for any suspicious char-
acters, Joe headed inland. The smoke scent grew
stronger. It was not long before he came to a small
clearing, in the center of which smoldered a campfire. Nobody was in sight.

The boy remained in concealment at the edge of
the forest a few minutes. Then he strode forward
and examined the ashes. The heat they still radi-
ated was mute evidence that somebody had been
there within the past few minutes. Was he the same

person who used the lean-to? If so, why did he build his campfire at such a distance from his shack?

"Maybe he went back there," Joe thought. "I'd better get back myself and find out."

As he started through the woods again, a gleaming object on the ground caught his eye just in time. It was a heavy trap, half-concealed by a frond of ferns, its steel jaws set for prey. The boy's foot had just missed it.

Joe bent down to examine the trap. Judging from the condition of the rabbit-meat bait, it must have been set recently.

Suddenly the youth had that eerie feeling that he was being spied upon. He glanced ahead just in time to see the head of a man duck out of sight in a near-by thicket. The stranger had light-colored hair and sharp eyes. Though Joe had caught only a quick glimpse of the face, he knew that he had seen it before.

"The salesman at the Morton farm!" he muttered.

Joe raced after the retreating man. The fugitive made no effort to conceal his trail as he crashed through the woods.

"He thinks he can outrun me," Joe told himself.

The stranger's flight paralleled the river but far enough inland to escape detection by anyone on the water.

Then suddenly the man turned and headed straight toward the edge of the river. Joe caught another fleeting glimpse of him as he dashed from stone to stone across a shallow ford just below a bend in the river, and disappeared into the woods on the opposite side.

Reasoning that it might be foolhardy to resume the chase alone, Joe gave a bird whistle that the Hardys often used between them as a signal. In a couple of seconds the whistle was repeated somewhere along the stream. Frank must have heard him, and was returning the signal.

Then a thought struck Joe. "Could this be an echo?"

Turning around, he whistled again. Once more the reply came, but this time from the woods across the water. It was not an echo. Joe dashed over the stones in the bed of the stream, hoping to find his brother on the other side.

He had barely reached the opposite bank when he caught sight of the running man directly ahead of him. In the same moment the fellow turned and recrossed the stream to the side from which they both had come.

The whistle came again. It was very clear.

"Frank must be close by," Joe thought, and plunged once more after the suspect.

CHAPTER X

A Cry for Help

IN THE meanwhile Frank and Chet had run into trouble. After shoving off to explore the river farther upstream, they had come to a stretch of the river where the water ran over a series of large underwater rocks.

So intent were they in looking for a sign of habitation along the shore that they did not notice a ledge of submerged rock until it was too late. The jagged ledge tore a gaping hole in the canvas a few feet behind the prow of the canoe. Water came pouring in.

"Here!" Frank shouted, as he whipped off his wool shirt. "Stuff this in the hole."

Chet caught the shirt and speedily plugged the opening. But water still gushed in. Chet yanked off his own shirt and wadded it in the torn canvas and smashed ribbing, while Frank strained at the crude paddle to drive the canoe ashore. Despite their efforts, water was halfway to the gunwales when the bow scraped the pebbly bottom of the left bank.

"Whew! Just made it!" Chet exclaimed. "But gosh, what am I going to do? I couldn't even get a good secondhand price for this tub now!"

"We'll take a look."

The boys hopped out, dragged the canoe up on the bank, and turned it over to examine the damage.

Chet groaned. "It never can be mended," he said forlornly. "Fifty smackers gone!"

"What do you mean? This canoe can be made as good as new by a repairman. In the meantime we'll use a patch of canvas and some waterproof adhesive from the pack," Frank told him.

The boys had nearly completed their temporary repair work when they heard a whistle. It was a long-drawn-out birdcall. The Hardy signal!

"Wait here!" Frank said to Chet.

He returned the whistle, then dashed downstream along the bank. Within a few seconds he found himself at a sharp bend in the river. The whistle sounded again! On which side of the water was Joe? He was not in sight, but the whistle was repeated. This time Frank was sure it had come from across the stream. Seeing a shallow place to cross just below him, he ran to it and splashed across. Joe was not there. Frank whistled. There was no reply.

"Where'd he go?" Frank wondered.

He hoped his brother was not in danger. But where to look for him was a question.

Frank decided to go back to Chet. Joe might have headed in that direction, too, or it was even possible Chet had returned the whistle.

Making his way quickly to the place where he had left the canoe, Frank found Chet just finishing the third sandwich he had brought.

"Didn't you find Joe?" he asked, wide-eyed.

"Not yet. Chet, did you give our whistle?"

"No. But I heard you two fellows signaling back and forth."

"The sound seemed to come from both sides of the stream," Frank replied, perplexed. "I hope it doesn't mean somebody was imitating our call."

Chet mopped his brow. "Gosh, if that happened, then the fellow who left the warning must be on our trail!" he exclaimed, glancing anxiously at the woods about him.

Suddenly his eyes were attracted by something rising above the treetops.

"Frank! Pigeons!"

Two white birds rose high, circled for several seconds, then headed south. A startling thought struck Frank. Were these pigeons from the same covey as the ones sent to the Hardy home? If his guess were correct, then the kidnapers might have their hide-out near this very spot!

Maybe Joe had stumbled on the men by accident and run into trouble!

As the two birds disappeared from view, another pair of pigeons came into sight. Like the others, they started to circle, when suddenly a blast cut the forest stillness and echoed and re-echoed through the trees.

"A shot!" Frank exclaimed.

Chet cried out, "One of the pigeons must have been winged!"

The bird wheeled, then plummeted through the trees, while the other soared away.

"I'm going to find out who fired that shot," Frank declared.

"Don't! Don't!" Chet pleaded. "He might shoot at you, too!"

"Joe may be held prisoner by that fellow," Frank said grimly. "I must find out."

"Then I'll go with you," Chet offered, and trailed behind Frank.

"That shot sounded no more than a couple of hundred feet away," Frank whispered. "Easy now."

As they stepped carefully from tree to tree to avoid presenting themselves as targets, Frank's attention was attracted to a red cylinder on the ground. He picked it up.

"Look, Chet, a shotgun shell!"

Chet surveyed the woodland with quickening pulse. Perhaps the bright barrel of a gun was being aimed at them that very second! He searched the area carefully, but he could see no one.

A score of paces farther on Frank found the pigeon, feathers ruffled, lying dead on a big boulder.

"It really caught a load of lead," he observed, lifting the limp, still warm body of the bird.

There were no bands of identification on the pigeon, nor a message tube. This fact strengthened Frank's suspicion that these birds, too, belonged to the criminals who had sent the ransom message.

He was relieved by the fact that there had been only one shot. At least Joe had not been under fire.

But presently Frank's imagination got the better of him. He visualized Joe being hustled off through the woods, his hands high in the air, and a shotgun prodding him in the back. Frank's reverie was brought to a sudden end by the spine-chilling howl of a dog, and the wild yell of a human being calling for help. Both sounds ended as suddenly as they had started.

"Th-that was Joe!" quavered Chet.

Frank did not reply. But with a furious burst of speed he dashed among the trees toward the direction from which the sound had come, unmindful of the brambles that tore at his clothes or the low-hanging branches that stung his cheeks. Chet panted after him as fast as his weight and the pack would allow.

Suddenly Frank found himself on a fairly well-beaten trail. He sped along it.

"Wait! Wait for me!" Chet cried.

The Hardy boy slackened his speed. Chet caught up to him at a spot where the trail cut through a dense growth of bushes.

"Come on!" Frank urged.

The two boys dashed among the bushes. A second later the ground seemed to drop away from beneath their feet.

Frank and Chet plunged helplessly downward!

CHAPTER XI

Foiling the Enemy

SLOWLY Frank Hardy opened his eyes. He was lying in a tangled mass of brush and sod.

"Where am I?" he said half aloud.

The boy moved his right hand and felt someone lying beside him. Then he sensed a crushing pressure on his legs.

Frank rubbed his hand over his forehead to clear his brain. Memory came back with a rush. He had been running with Chet. Then that awful drop. Now he found himself lying at the bottom of a deep pit.

Summoning every ounce of strength in his body, the boy raised himself up on one elbow. In the gloom of the pit he peered at the body beside him.

"Joe!" he cried hoarsely.

His brother lay there, unconscious or . . . Frank caught his breath. Dismissing this terrible thought from his mind, Frank grabbed Joe's hand. It moved. He was alive!

In trying to rise, Frank realized that the weight on his legs was Chet. His friend's knees were doubled up under his chin and he did not budge.

Frank rumpled the boy's hair. "Chet! Chet! Are you all right?"

In a few seconds Chet's eyes opened and the dazed look disappeared from them.

"Where are we? How did we get here?" he asked in bewilderment.

"We plunged into a pit of some kind. Here's Joe."

"Joe? How'd he—" Then Chet realized that Joe was unconsious.

"We've got to get him out of here," said Frank. The pit into which they had fallen was deep and narrow. Frank and Chet had trouble worming their way to a standing position. As Frank bent down to place his hands beneath his brother's shoulders, Joe stirred. He shook his head dazedly, and tried to sit up.

"Attaboy," Frank said. "Take it easy. You had quite a bang."

"Oh, that dog," Joe groaned. "It nearly had me."

"What dog?" Chet asked.

"The one that chased me." Joe looked around.

In a few seconds his mind cleared completely. "Oh, yes, I fell in here. It's a good thing you two found me."

"We didn't find you," Chet said with a rueful grin. "We dropped in on you!"

"What do you mean?"

"We toppled into this hole, too," Frank explained.

"Well, let's get out of it before anybody else has a hankering to visit us," Joe pleaded, although he felt pretty weak.

"Golly, it's eight feet deep if it's an inch," Chet moaned.

"Climb on my shoulders, Chet," Frank suggested. "Once you're topside you can haul us up."

"Look out for snipers," Joe warned.

Although Chet did not relish the thought of meeting one of their enemies, he obediently climbed to Frank's shoulders and stood up on his teetering perch, with Frank grasping the stout boy's ankles to steady him. Chet peered around. Seeing no one, he wriggled over the top.

"Ready?" he called down.

"Okay."

As Frank braced himself again, Joe sprang up. In a moment he, too, was out of the pit. With Joe helping Chet keep his balance, the stout boy pulled Frank from the hole.

The three of them sprawled on the ground to get their breath back and to take stock of their injuries. They were relieved to find that aside from a few minor scratches and bruises all were unhurt.

"What were you doing way off here?" Frank asked his brother.

Joe told about the steel trap in which he had nearly caught his foot, then of spotting the man who had probably set it.

"What did he look like?"

"Tall and blond. I couldn't see his face very distinctly except for his eyes. But I knew that I had seen him before. I'm pretty certain that he's the same guy who followed you from the newspaper office and who posed as a salesman that morning at Chet's farm."

"Ow-ee, I don't like this," the stout boy said. "Then where'd he go?"

"After he saw me he started to run. He sure led me a chase across the river and back. I whistled for you, Frank."

In comparing notes the brothers found each of them had whistled only twice. So the stranger *had* imitated them!

"Just to lead me on," Joe declared. "I was a goon to fall for it!"

"What was it you said about a dog?" Chet asked. "We heard one howl."

"And what a howl!" Joe said. "I yelled for help!"

He added that just before he had pitched into the hole, the ferocious beast had come crashing through the woods and raced after him.

"One of the wild dogs of North Woods!" Chet exclaimed. "I knew they'd get us!"

"He didn't quite get me," Joe said, "but it was a close race. Maybe it was a good thing I fell into this hole!"

"Holy crow!" Frank exclaimed, as a thought suddenly occurred to him. "Do you realize this hole was covered with brush when Chet and I fell in?"

"N-never thought of that," Chet said. "Then somebody sneaked up after Joe was trapped and covered it up again!"

"Right. Maybe the idea was to catch all three of us and then . . ."

"He may be coming back to capture us right now," Chet said, struggling to his feet. "Let's leave, pronto."

Ordinarily, the Hardys would not have given up their efforts to solve the puzzling problem they had set out to untangle, but physically they were in no shape to proceed. They were badly in need of food and rest before they would be able to take up their search of the missing rifles and to find out what mischief the pseudo salesman was up to and why everybody was so determined to keep them out of the North Woods.

As the boys worked their way back to the canoe, Chet told Joe how it had rammed a rock and how they had made temporary repairs. Suddenly a grim thought struck him. "I'll bet you my next meal the canoe and pack are gone," he said.

Fearing there might be something to this dire prediction, the Hardys quickened their pace.

"It's a long hike back to the other fellows," Chet moaned. "It would be dark before we could get to camp, and these gangsters—"

At that moment the boys reached the bank of the stream and Joe called out: "Chet, you were wrong. The canoe is still here!"

"Whew!" breathed Chet, vastly relieved.

"I hope you're not hungry," Joe said to him, "because you lost your bet. Frank and I will divvy your next meal."

"Oh, no you won't!" said Chet, smiling ruefully. "I was only kidding."

"A bet's a bet," Frank reminded him.

The boys quickly surveyed the patched canoe. "Not bad!" Joe said approvingly.

"If we don't hit any more rocks, I guess we can make camp."

They shoved off, taking the same positions as they

had on the trip up. It was easier traveling with the current. Keeping a sharp lookout for underwater rocks, the Hardys deftly steered the canoe while Chet sat relaxed in the bottom, his hands behind his head.

"Oh, brother," he burst out, "I hope Biff and Tony have chow ready. I'm dying of hunger."

"Forget it," Joe said. "No supper for you. It'll be good for your waistline. What is it now? About a quarter of a mile around?"

"Cut it," Chet begged. "A guy's got to eat."

"We might save you one pickle," Frank offered placatingly.

Chet cast a sidewise glance at Frank. The Hardy boy certainly looked as if he meant it about the bet. Chet decided that if he changed the subject, perhaps they would forget about it.

"How large was the dog that chased you, Joe?" he asked.

"About four feet long. It sure looked like a wolf."

"A wild dog is as fierce as a wolf, my Uncle Ty says," Chet spoke up. "They're killers."

Joe said he had a hunch that the dog might belong to the blond man, who probably called him off after seeing Joe fall.

Frank recounted his and Chet's experiences, ending with the pigeon episode.

"At least one thing begins to look certain," he

said in conclusion. "The thieves who stole Chet's truck were also my kidnapers or at least they're in cahoots with them."

"It wouldn't surprise me," Joe said, "if their headquarters aren't far from here."

Chet winced. Then suddenly he beamed. "Hey, fellows, I see camp!" he announced. A tantalizing aroma filled the air. "Food!" he exclaimed as the canoe grounded on the shore close by the camp.

Biff and Tony, seeing their friends' bruises and disheveled clothes, fired questions in rapid succession, growing more amazed as each was answered.

"Those men sure must want to keep people away from these parts," Tony remarked.

"You might have been killed," Biff said, his jaw tensing. "A man has to be pretty desperate to build a deadfall to capture someone who's never done him any harm."

The boys conjectured about what underhanded schemes the pit digger might be carrying on, but could figure out nothing except that for one reason or another he wanted to prevent people from entering a certain section of the woods.

"Tomorrow we'll track him down and find out!" Frank said with determination, as he put some ointment on a leg bruise. "We're really on their trail now, and we must be getting mighty close to their hangout."

He restored the ointment to his pack, and made his way toward the campfire. Tony, who was an expert outdoor chef, had a stew simmering in an open pot.

"Get in the chow line!" Biff shouted.

"All but Chet," Joe spoke up, winking at Biff. "Frank and I won his share on a bet."

"Wh-what—you don't mean it!" Chet moaned, his eyes bulging.

"How about scouting around and looking for that guy who left us the warning while we eat?" Joe suggested. "It will take your mind off your appetite."

Mumbling that he would never make another bet in his life, but determined to be a good sport, Chet made for the shore of the pond. His friends looked at one another. How long should they make him suffer? They let him get out of sight, then Frank called:

"Hey, Chet, come back! You forgot something!"

The stout boy did not return, however. At first they thought he was miffed, and went on eating without him. When ten minutes had gone by and Chet had not returned, Frank began to worry about him. This was not at all like Chet.

CHAPTER XII

The Detector

"THINK I'll take a look and see what Chet's up to," Frank said, setting down his tin plate.

"Oh, enjoy yourself," Biff advised, as he reached for a second helping. "Maybe Chet'll solve our mystery for us on his empty stomach."

"He certainly ought to," Tony spoke up. "It's his stuff that was stolen."

Frank waited another couple of minutes. Then he whistled. No answer. He called Chet's name, saying they were saving some chow for him. But there was no response.

"Chet may not be able to answer," Frank said. "I'll take a look."

The other boys were inclined to think that Chet was swimming in the pond or looking for food— berries, edible leaves, sassafras. This was one department in which he was an expert.

For several minutes Frank searched without finding a trace of his stout friend. Then suddenly he saw him on the far side of the pond, a fish pole in his hands. He was just baiting it. After he had cast, Frank came up behind him.

Chet looked up and grinned. "Caught one already."

"Where'd you get the swell pole?" Frank asked.

"Found it. Pretty nifty, eh? Practically new. Think I'll—"

Chet jumped as he realized that under the circumstances this pole meant more than its loss by a careless fisherman. It might be the property of the fellow who left the warning the night before.

"Gosh, I never thought—I was so hungry—I'd better—"

Frank grinned. "Might as well let the fish bite," he advised. "There's not much stew left."

A tug came on Chet's line and two minutes later he had landed a sleek perch.

"Any identification on that pole?" Frank asked.

Chet looked. "Say, Frank, this rod came from Wells Hardware Store. Here's the name."

"I'm sure the owner didn't mean to leave it," Frank observed as the boys walked back. "You know, Chet, this might be a means of finding out what the thief looks like."

"How?"

"I'll bet he was buying this rod when you were

in the store. He may have heard you talking to the clerk. Right?"

Chet admitted he had bragged about his big-game-hunter uncle and the rifles in the truck. There were several customers in the store at the time, but he had paid no attention to them.

"Gee, if I only had!" he said ruefully.

Frank thought there was a good chance the mysterious fisherman would return for the pole during the night, and suggested they stay on watch to nab him.

Reaching camp, Chet displayed the pole and his catch. Joe handed him a plate of stew. "Eat," he commanded, "before you fall into a dead faint!"

Chet mumbled his thanks. As he went to work with knife and fork, the other boys talked about the various phases of the mystery. How many thieves were involved, and what were the boys' chances of recovering the stolen equipment?

"Pretty poor, I'd say," was Tony's comment. "What could we do against a stack of rifles?"

"Anyway, we won't be in danger of a surprise attack," Frank said. "After this, we'll use the sound detector we brought. Good thing you thought of it, Joe."

"I didn't know you had one," Tony said.

"The gadget belongs to Dad, but he lets us borrow it."

Frank opened his pack and drew out the detector. It was only the size of a cigarette case, but one could plainly hear sounds far beyond the ear range. During the late afternoon and evening the boys took turns listening.

"You could almost hear the guys breathe with this gimmick," Tony said gleefully. "It's swell!"

No sounds of particular interest were picked up, and at nine o'clock Frank replaced the detector in his pack.

"Think I'll hit the sack," he told the others.

"Me, too," said Joe. "Biff, arrange the watches, will you?"

After two-hour shifts had been agreed upon, Biff turned on his radio for news of the missing Jack Wayne. The announcer said there was still no clue to the whereabouts of the pilot, although the search was still being carried on over the ocean.

"That means they've given up looking around here," said Joe, wriggling into his bag. "I—ugh!" He withdrew his legs like lightning.

"What's the matter?" Biff asked.

"A snake."

Joe reached for his light and a long stick. Flashing the beam into his sleeping bag, he probed it carefully. Out came a string of frankfurters!

Chet burst out laughing. "I didn't want you to

go to bed hungry," he said. "Tony, can you still cook those weenies?"

"Okay," Joe said with a grin. "We're square now, Chet."

The boys fell asleep with Biff left on guard. Frank took his turn in the early morning. So far there had been no prowlers. Soon a rosy tint covered the eastern heavens.

"We should get started on our sleuthing soon," he told himself an hour later, as he prepared three small emergency kits with knives, rope, first-aid articles, and some food.

He roused the others, and it was not long before he, Joe, and Biff had had breakfast and were ready to shove off in the canoe. Chet and Tony would remain at camp in case anyone should show up for the fishing pole.

As the other boys started off, a light mist rose from the river and drifted among the trees on shore. By the time the sun had burned the mist away, they had reached the spot where Chet and Frank had seen the pigeons the day before. They decided to start operations from there.

"We'd better hide this canoe well," Joe advised. "Give me a hand, Biff."

The two boys carried the craft a hundred feet inland and concealed it in a thicket.

"Now what?" Biff asked.

"Let's start from the pit and work north," Joe suggested. "That blond fellow I followed was headed in that direction."

They started forward cautiously. Frank turned on the sound detector and listened intently. Birdcalls, insect sounds, he reported, but no human voices. In a short time the hikers came to the trail which led to the pit. As they neared it, Joe called excitedly:

"The hole's covered over again! Watch out, Biff! Don't take a swan dive into it as we did yesterday."

The pit was well camouflaged. Brush and sod had been piled so naturally over it that unless one knew its exact location he would have difficulty finding it.

"I think the hole's been covered recently," Frank said, pointing to a freshly heeled cigarette butt alongside it.

He put the detector to his ear. No sounds came from it except those of woodland creatures and the distant murmur of the stream.

Spreading out twenty feet apart, the boys moved along silently. Frank stopped every few seconds to listen.

Then suddenly the youth raised his hand for the

others to stop. "I hear something different, but it's very faint," he called.

Extremely careful not to make any noise, the boys followed him in the direction of the mysterious sound which the instrument had registered. A hundred feet farther he halted again.

"You take this gadget, Joe, and tell me what you think it is."

Joe listened. "Something's pounding or hammering," he said.

"I thought it might be a machine," Frank said. "You listen, Biff."

After holding the detector to his ear a few seconds the lanky youth grinned. "I don't hear anything like that. You fellows spoofing me?"

Joe grabbed the instrument. "That's right. The sound has stopped."

Frank frowned. "Maybe we've been seen. From now on we'd better creep along," he advised.

"Yeah, we may be right on top of their hide-out," Biff said grimly.

The ground ahead rose slightly to the crown of a little hillock. Reaching the top, the boys peered hopefully down the other side.

"Do you see what I see?" Frank whispered excitedly. "Isn't that a chimney sticking up behind those trees? Come on, fellows!"

The boys made their way down the hill, taking extreme care to keep well concealed.

"Let's sneak up on the place from three directions." This from Biff.

The chimney belonged to an old tumble-down shack. The roof was half caved in, and gunny sacks were nailed over the windows.

"Guess nobody lives here," Biff observed.

"Somebody may be hiding in it, though," said Frank. "We'd better find out."

The boys conferred briefly on making a surprise attack. It was decided that Joe would throw a rock at the back of the cabin. If anybody were inside, his attention would be directed there. Then Frank and Biff would rush in through the front door.

Well hidden in the bushes, Joe selected a large stone. Taking careful aim, he sent it sailing toward the building. It hit with a startling crash. Immediately Frank and Biff raced from cover and ran through the front entrance.

Nobody was inside. The only sign of habitation was a rickety cot, which showed no evidence of recent use. On a crude hearth lay a heap of ashes. Frank felt the stones. They were cold. By this time Joe, too, had entered the place.

"Nobody home," Biff announced.

"What's that?" Joe asked, as he noticed a large object, draped with burlap bags, standing in a corner. He pulled them off, revealing a large motor.

"Great cow!" he exclaimed. "It's an airplane engine. How did it get here?"

An idea flashed into Biff's mind. "The missing plane! Maybe it crashed in these woods after all and somebody dragged the motor here!"

"It couldn't have been dragged far," Joe said excitedly. "This thing is heavy. I'll bet Jack Wayne's near by. Come on, fellows, let's look for him!"

CHAPTER XIII

A Hoax

By the time the boys had raced fifty feet, reason returned to them.

"If Jack Wayne crashed here," Frank said, "the person who moved the motor would have taken care of him, too."

"The gang," Joe guessed. "Maybe that's what Wayne meant by 'pirate.'"

Biff had a different idea. "Wayne may not be here at all. That motor could have torn loose from the plane before it crashed."

Frank ran back into the cabin. "Hey!" he called out excitedly. "This motor has never been in a plane. It's brand new! I should have noticed that right away!"

"How do you suppose they ever got a big, heavy airplane engine through all these woods?" asked Joe. "We had trouble enough just with our packs!"

The three boys scouted around the area for further evidence, agreeing to meet again at the cabin to report any sign of a plane accident or other unusual circumstance. Joe, the first to return, had seen nothing unusual, except that a piece of bark had been chipped off a tree standing near the shack.

Wondering if the cut had any special import, he looked at other trees in the vicinity. Three of them had had bits of bark stripped off.

Joe was about to look farther, when Frank and Biff joined him. After hearing they had failed to locate a crack-up, he called their attention to the nicked trees.

"I believe they're trail blaze marks," he said, "and made not very long ago. Let's follow 'em and see where they lead to."

Within five minutes two other marked trees were found. There was no question but that a trail was indicated.

"Do you think it might lead to the wrecked plane?" Biff asked.

The Hardys could not see why anyone would mark a trail for this reason, and were inclined to believe the trail might possibly take them near the hide-out of the men they were seeking. The boys continued to follow it.

The Hardys' keen eyes kept alert for any evidence

that the thieves or kidnapers might be around. By midmorning Biff was weary from following the blazed trees with no end to the trail.

"Say, fellows," he sighed, "how far do we go with this search?"

The Hardys had to admit things looked rather hopeless. Frank kept listening to his detector, but if the forest held a secret, it was being kept well.

All at once Biff let out a cry. "Well, what do you know about this? We've been going in a circle."

Frank and Joe rushed to where the boy stood. There was no doubt about it. An oak with some of its bark removed was easily identified by a long split down the trunk into which a bird had built a nest.

Following a trampled path, the boys found another familiar tree, then another. Biff scratched his head.

"I don't see why anybody would mark a trail in a circle," he said.

After a few minutes' thought, Frank suggested that there probably were offshoots of the main trail. The boys spread out to look. Only Biff found one.

"This thing's got me dizzy," he said. "Where are we headed, anyway?"

Frank pulled his compass from his pocket, then grinned. "Even this is stuck," he said.

By Joe's compass the new trail would lead them

east, but a moment later twin pines with part of their bark removed turned the boys south.

Frank stopped. "I'm beginning to think there's something phony about this whole deal," he said. "Maybe this trail was made on purpose to lead people away from the cabin or the place where we heard the hammering sound."

"You mean I'm going to fall into some trap the way you fellows did?" Biff exclaimed, frowning.

"Not if you watch your step," Joe replied.

The boys walked on. More trail marks, and more unfamiliar territory. Silence followed, until Frank said:

"I've picked up something on the detector, fellows. Sounds like digging. Somebody's up ahead, and not far away!"

The hikers dropped to the ground, then crept slowly forward, inching their way so as not to show themselves or to make any noise.

"Do you suppose the thieves are burying loot?" Biff whispered. In his enthusiasm to make a capture he outdistanced the others.

Ahead loomed a large rock. The unknown digger was on the other side of it. The boys now could hear the sound of metal biting into the soil.

"Here goes!" Biff told himself.

He raised up and flung himself upon the stooped figure. There was a tangle of arms and legs. The digger was overpowered. Biff peered into his face.

"Chet! Well, I'll be mousetrapped," he blurted, rising from the stout boy's midriff.

"What are you doing here?" Frank asked.

"Yes, how did you get this far from camp?" Joe put in eagerly.

"W-w-wait a minute," Chet begged. "Let me catch my breath. You guys make me sick, always playing jokes. What do you think I am, a tackling dummy?"

He sat down against the rock and mopped his brow. "I do a fellow a favor," he continued, "and this is what happens."

"Do whom a favor?" Frank asked.

"Tony. Who else?" Chet puffed. "I'm digging worms for him. He wants to catch some trout."

The boys looked down at the hole. Chet had been digging it with his tin plate. Two worms wriggled beside it.

"Where's Tony?" Frank asked.

"At camp. Right over there!"

"Oh, no!" Joe wailed. "Not that!"

"Sure. Didn't you know?" Chet rose and slapped the dust from his pants.

"Jumpin' jeepers!" Biff exclaimed. "Somebody made a trail right here to our camp!"

"And somebody devilishly clever!" Frank said. "I believe he did it to keep an eye on us."

"He probably was watching all the time," Biff declared. "But if he was one of the gang, why didn't he just shoot at us and get it over with?"

"I don't think the trail was made by one of the gang," Frank said. "We may have a friend in North Woods."

"What do you mean?" Chet asked.

"That warning note we received may have been left by someone with good intentions, and he's helped us out again."

After Chet heard the whole story, he said, "Two warnings are enough for me. I vote we leave this place."

"I think Chet's right," Biff said. "Let's shove off."

Tony agreed with Chet and Biff.

"What's more," he said, "my dad's expecting me home to drive for him."

Outvoted, the Hardys agreed to go, but begged the others to stay until morning.

"Look, fellows," Frank said, "Joe and I will do some work alone. You fellows stay here and swim. Besides, we have to get the canoe."

They ate a quick lunch from the emergency kit they were carrying, then followed the marked trees all the way back to the tumble-down shack. They approached it quietly and stepped inside, Frank in the lead.

"Joe! The motor's gone!"

The boys stared in amazement at the spot where the engine had stood. The burlap sacks had been tossed to one side.

"Gosh, I wish I'd taken the serial number of that engine," Joe said.

"I wonder how much of a gang is in on this deal," Frank mused. "It would take several strong men to move that heavy engine. Well, now where do we head?"

The brothers decided to depend on the detector for help. Finally their patience bore fruit.

"Hammering?" Joe asked as his brother's face lighted up.

"No."

"The wailing siren?"

Frank shook his head. "An animal."

Joe listened. "Maybe it's the dog that attacked me," he said.

"If he belongs to that fake salesman, now's our chance to find that crook!" Frank vowed.

Hunting knives in hand to assist in any unexpected attack, the boys started off in the direction of the howling, which now could be heard without the aid of the detector.

"That's more than one animal," Frank said.

The Hardys proceeded more slowly. Suddenly a clearing opened up ahead. In the middle of it the boys saw a six-foot wire enclosure. Behind the netting five animals growled fiercely.

"Wolves!" Joe exclaimed.

"Sure looks that way," Frank answered.

"What are they doing here?"

"We'll find out."

Careful to keep themselves concealed, the boys circled the enclosure. The wolves smelled their presence, however, and started to howl.

"I hope they haven't given us away," Joe whispered. "Their keeper must be near by."

The boys looked about them. Partly concealed among the trees some distance to their left was a cabin, its front door open.

The brothers approached it cautiously. Nobody was in sight.

"Someone may be spying on us from a window," Joe whispered.

He and Frank waited a few minutes before approaching closer to the cabin. Nothing seemed to be stirring.

"I'm going to take a look," Joe said.

"I'm with you."

They stepped quietly through the brush and into a small open space in front of the cabin. There was an ominous silence about the place.

Anxiety showed on Frank's face. "Joe, I don't like . . ."

His words were punctured by a snarl which froze the boys in their tracks. The head of a wolf dog flashed in the doorway. With a vicious growl, the animal sprang toward the Hardys.

"The same dog!" thought Joe, poising his knife.

Suddenly the dog let out a piercing whine and jerked back. Then the boys saw that he was chained to the door. Picking himself up, the frustrated animal continued to bellow and glower, straining at his leash.

A sharp voice cut the air. *"Stand where you are!"* The words sounded as savage as the wolf dog's cry.

Frank and Joe wheeled. A tall man, his hat pulled low, stood before them, a gun in his hand.

CHAPTER XIV

A Strange Pet

THE man was a giant of a woodsman. His face was heavily bearded and his eyes fiercely sharp. Besides the gun, he carried a long whip.

"What are you doing here?" he demanded.

"Oh—uh—just looking around," Frank replied, trying to look innocent. "I'm afraid we're lost."

The man eyed the boys sharply, as if he doubted this statement.

"You're trespassing on private property," he said sternly.

"Private?" Joe asked.

"Yes. I breed wolves here. This is a dangerous area."

All the while the animal chained to the door growled and pulled at his leash.

"Quiet, Saber!" the man shouted.

He flicked his whip and the end of it snapped like a rifle shot a scant two inches from the wolf dog's jaws. The animal retreated and threw itself down across the doorway.

"Are your wolves timber wolves?" Joe asked, sparring for time.

The keeper opened his mouth in a roaring laugh. "Timber wolves? And I suppose you think Saber is just an ordinary dog." He laughed again. "My wolves are real Siberian wolves, boy. Man-killers. If I should let Saber loose on you . . . Ho-ho-ho!"

"Why do you keep such ferocious beasts?"

"I breed them for the zoos. My animals are always in demand."

"How do you transport them out of here?" Joe queried.

The man gave the boy a suspicious glance. "That's my business," he snapped. "And now I want to give you kids some good advice. Leave this forest pronto and don't come back! Do you hear me? *Don't come back!*"

Frank was not ready to go quite yet. This man might know some things the Hardys wanted to find out.

"Do you take care of these animals all alone?" he asked.

"Yes."

"Oh, by the way, we found a valuable rod and reel near our camp down near the river. Do you know who may have left it there?"

"No."

"Did a plane crash around here recently?" Joe queried.

"No."

"There's an old shack off in the woods," Frank said, pointing to the direction from which they had come. "Anybody live there?"

"Listen, I ain't answering any more of your nebby questions," the woodsman said curtly. "Now clear out of here and don't let me see you around these parts again!" He cracked his whip. "Get going!"

Joe thrust out his chin in determination. "We'll go," he said, "but we don't intend to be ordered around like animals!"

The man merely glared as the boys retreated into the woods, following the trail over which they had come. When they were out of earshot of him, they stopped to talk over the situation.

"I sure don't care for that fellow!" Joe said slowly.

"Same here. I wouldn't trust him as far as I could throw a haystack," Frank agreed. "And his story about breeding wolves for zoos sounded awfully fishy."

"The dog that chased me just before I fell into the pit," Joe said, "looked an awful lot like Saber. I'll bet it was Saber."

"Listen!" Frank said suddenly.

In the distance he had detected the sound of something crashing through the brush.

"Saber!" Joe exclaimed. "The woodsman's let him loose!"

"Up a tree!" Frank warned.

The brothers raced through the forest until they spotted a couple of fir trees they could climb readily. Leaping to the lowest branches, they pulled themselves up into the trees.

They were barely a safe distance off the ground when Saber reached them. Snarling and snapping, he pawed at one tree trunk and then the other. Joe broke off a branch and hurled it down, hitting the wolf dog on the nose. The infuriated animal howled and ran in circles around the tree.

"This beast may not let us down for days," Joe remarked woefully.

"There's one way we can catch him," Frank said hopefully. "With a pole and noose."

"The way they bring 'em back alive in Africa?"

"Right. Say, there's a branch above you that's pretty straight."

Joe climbed up. He cut off the branch and quickly stripped it of twigs and leaves.

"I have a coil of small rope in my pocket," Frank said, pulling it out.

He threw it across to Joe, who fastened a noose to the end of the pole.

"This is going to be risky," Frank warned. "Don't let him pull you off your perch."

Joe dangled the pole and the noose close to the ground. The wolf dog snapped at it. With a deft twist, the boy flung the rope over Saber's head. "Pull!" Frank cried.

The boy hauled the pole upward, but the dog was heavy. It lashed about fiercely, snarling and gnashing with its fangs. Suddenly the animal freed itself and tumbled to the ground.

"Whew!" Joe exclaimed. "He weighs a ton."

Saber continued to circle the trees but more warily. Joe tried to rope him again, but the wolf dog would not be tricked the second time.

As the boys wondered what to do, they were startled by a distant wailing noise.

"What's that, Frank? The siren?"

"Sounds like it, but it's mighty faint."

"Well, what do you know about that?" Joe cried. "The dog's leaving!"

The strange sound seemed to bother the animal. Putting its tail between its legs, Saber slunk off.

"He acts frightened. My guess is that the sound hurts his ears."

The boys dropped to the ground. "Gosh, I thought I was going to have to live in that tree." Joe grinned, as he stretched his legs. "Let's get back to camp."

The Hardys found their way to the spot where the canoe was cached. They slid it into the water and paddled rapidly downstream. By the time they had rejoined the other boys, the sun was sinking behind the trees to the west.

Chet, Biff, and Tony rushed to the shore to meet their companions.

"Any luck on my stolen stuff?" Chet asked.

"Did you locate the gang's hide-out?" Tony asked excitedly.

"We were treed by a wolf dog," Joe said.

"Oh, stumped again," Biff said, thinking Joe was kidding.

"Quit your wisecracks, Biff," Tony said. "Let's listen to what the fellows have to say."

As Frank and Joe related their adventures, Chet's mouth sagged open.

"W-wolves?" he asked in disbelief. "And a wolf dog! If he picks up our scent, he'll come right into this camp. What say, fellows, let's get out of here!"

Frank and Joe felt fairly sure that even if Saber had picked up their trail he would get no farther than the place they had put the canoe into the water.

"But to make sure he doesn't bother us again, we'll have to catch the critter," Joe said determinedly.

"With our bare hands, I suppose," Biff retorted.

"No. With a stockade. We'll build one after

chow. How about it, Tony? Do we have trout to-night?"

"Six nice fat Rainbows," was the proud answer. "Biff and I caught 'em."

"With my worms," Chet added.

The boys laughed and joked through the meal. When it was over, Frank said:

"Now to work on the stockade. We'll need saplings—plenty of 'em."

A number of small trees grew along the stream and the boys made short work of felling them. Soon, a pile of saplings, stripped of their branches, lay on the spot which the Hardys had selected for the trap.

While the others were fashioning a small trench, Joe and Frank went into the woods for vines with which to tie the saplings together. They emerged with several handfuls of trailing vines.

Working rapidly, it did not take the boys long to erect a crude stockade. Frank arranged a small opening on one side with a door made of short saplings, which would drop in place once an animal had entered the trap.

"Now all we need is bait," Joe said. "Hey, Chet, you . . ."

"Don't look at me that way," Chet glared. "You're not going to use me—"

"I was only going to ask you to scare up a couple of rabbits," Joe said, grinning.

"I have a piece of meat left that we won't need," Tony said. "We can use that." He produced a sizable chunk left over from the piece which the boys had taken along for stew.

"That's perfect," Frank said.

He fastened the meat to a long string, which, when pulled, would cause the door to fall shut. They tried it several times to be sure the trap would work.

"Saber ought to tackle this meat before he does us," Joe said. "I hope this trap's strong enough to hold him. I don't want to be his dessert."

The site of the trap was some distance from the camp, but the boys could observe it from where they sat around the fire exchanging observations on the day's events. When darkness began to fall, Joe got up and stretched, yawning sleepily.

"I'm going to tumble in, fellows," he said. "I'll take a morning watch."

"Me, too," Biff yawned.

As Joe rose from the ground, he cried hoarsely, "Fellows, the stockade!"

All heads swung to the direction of the trap where two glowing eyes moved slowly toward the doorway.

"Ow!" Chet cried. "I'm holing up!" He made a dash for his sleeping bag and crawled in.

CHAPTER XV

Another Theft

No SOONER had Chet dived into his sack than the boys heard the corral gate drop. This was followed by a howling so wild and terrifying that the forest itself seemed to shudder.

"We've caught a wolf!" Joe exclaimed.

Biff and Tony started running toward the stockade.

"Easy," Frank warned. "Let the beast tire himself out before we take a look."

Excitedly, the boys stood by while the trapped animal thrashed about. It jumped at the walls of the stockade, making the saplings quiver under each assault. But they held fast. Finally the wolf's rage subsided into snarling submission.

"All right, now," Frank said. "We'll take a look at what we caught."

Beaming their flashlights ahead of them, the boys

warily approached the stockade. When they reached the side of it, Joe dropped down on hands and knees.

"Stand on my back," he said to Frank, "and take a gander over the top."

Carefully Frank trained his flash and peered down from the top of the sapling wall. A large wolf dog, a heavy collar around its neck, crouched in one corner of the stockade. Its tongue hung out and foam flecked the cruel mouth.

"Saber!" Frank cried out. "The woodsman's watchdog that treed us this afternoon. I'd know him anywhere."

The boys took turns looking down at the trembling animal.

"Th-that's the thing which chased you and Joe?" Chet said to Frank. "Boy, am I glad I stayed in camp!"

"What are we going to do with it?" Biff asked.

He received no immediate answer because Frank and Joe were conferring in low tones near the gate of the stockade.

"We don't have the upper hand here by a long shot," Frank was saying.

"I see what you mean," Joe replied. "Saber's master is probably near by."

"Right. If only he wasn't armed! We're no match against a man with a gun, Joe."

The boys decided to put on an act for the benefit of Saber's owner. In a loud voice Frank called out:

"Fellows, let's get out of here! This woods is no place for campers, even with Saber out of circulation."

"We'll go at the crack of dawn," Joe agreed vociferously. "I don't like the idea of being chewed up." Then he whispered to his brother, "But we'll come back here without that woodsman knowing about it. Maybe we'll have better luck next time."

Guard duty was arranged. Chet drew the first hour. As he sat propped against a tree, the youth mulled over the whole situation. He was torn between a desire to leave as early as possible, and a regret that the stolen rifles and other property had not been found. He hated to face his Uncle Ty. Moreover, there were weeks of farm work ahead of him before he could make restitution for the lost guns and camping equipment.

Chet gave a tremendous sigh. "Anyway, I got the canoe back," he said. "And the fellows have been using it," he thought, brightening, "so of course they'll help pay for that."

At breakfast he brought up the subject to the others. There was no reply. Chet repeated his plea. Finally Tony said:

"Haven't we been working hard enough for you? Nearly eaten alive, falling into pits—"

Chet subsided, but planned to try again as soon as they got safely out of the woods.

It was decided that he, Tony, and Biff would take the canoe and most of the camp equipment downstream. The river must eventually flow into the sea, probably near Barmet Bay.

"Joe and I'll hike back through the woods," Frank said. "We'll pick up the car, and contact you when we arrive home."

"What shall we do about Saber?" Joe asked. "We don't dare let him out, but we can't leave him to starve."

"We ought to put that beast out of the way," Frank said grimly, "but we'd better not. I'll bet that as soon as we go, his owner will come for him."

The Hardys shoved the laden canoe from shore and watched until their companions had paddled out of sight. Then they slung their packs over their shoulders and started back for the farm where they had left Chet's jalopy.

They had been on their way only a few minutes when Joe said, "Let's go back and have one more look. Are you game?"

Caching their packs in a thicket, the boys cautiously retraced their steps until they came to a big rock on a rise of ground. Peering around it, they were able to look down at the stockade. All was quiet except for the low growl of the wolf dog. But as the boys watched, the animal suddenly grew restless, its growl climbing the scale to a thin whine.

"He hears somebody," Frank said.

"Us, maybe?"

"No. I think that whine means his master is around."

Suddenly the brothers heard the distant sound of someone approaching through the brush and flattened themselves on the ground to escape detection. Whoever it was was making no effort to conceal his presence, certain that the campers had departed. The tramping of feet became louder, and a figure approached the stockade.

"The woodsman!" Joe whispered.

The bearded man stopped, listened, then went to the door of the stockade. Bending down, he lifted it, and when Saber's head appeared, he snapped a wire leash onto the animal's collar.

"Fool!" the boys heard the woodsman snarl. "Letting yourself get trapped by a bunch of kids." Then he cuffed the animal, which cringed at his feet. The vicious wolf dog acted like a beaten puppy.

The man retreated a few paces from the stockade and stood glaring at it. Then he ran up and hurled his body full force against the saplings. They began to give way under the charge.

He repeated the performance and at length the wall crashed in. Angrily the man continued to batter the stockade until it was level with the ground. Not until then did he set off with Saber.

"Whew!" Joe said when the man was out of sight. "Some temper! Well, let's make tracks! We know now that the wolf dog won't starve."

It was late in the afternoon before the Hardys reached the road where they had entered the woods. From there they went straight to the farmhouse and retrieved the jalopy. After thanking the farm woman for letting them park there, the brothers hopped in and started for home.

When they pulled up in front of their house shortly afterward, they found Chet sitting on the front steps, a piece of cake in one hand, a banana in the other.

"Hi, fellows!" he called out. "Got a lift into town, so I thought I'd pick up the jalopy."

Chet said the trip down the stream had been uneventful. It had joined the Willow River, which emptied into the bay. Tony had telephoned his home from a water-front restaurant, and Mrs. Prito had come to pick up the campers in her husband's small truck, and had delivered Chet and his canoe to the Morton home.

As soon as Chet had finished his cake he decided to drive home. The two tired boys picked up their packs, mounted the front porch steps, and entered the house. Mrs. Hardy flung her arms around them.

"I'm so glad you're back," she said. "Chet has been telling us the wildest kind of tales about man-killing wolves and prison pits and—"

She was interrupted by Aunt Gertrude who hustled into the hall from the kitchen. "I'm glad you're back safe, too. But that Morton boy! I'd like to tie his tongue up, scaring your mother with such preposterous stories. I sent him outside with some food to stop his talking. Man-killing wolves in North Woods! Ridiculous! Why, there isn't a man-killing wolf outside of Siberia, except in a few zoos."

Frank and Joe looked at each other. Perhaps they had better not tell the whole story of what had happened, except to their father. Learning that he was working on a report in his study, the brothers took the steps two at a time and burst in on him.

"Hello, sons," he said, smiling, and closed the door. "Now let's have the truth about your trip."

When the boys had finished a complete account of their adventures, the amazed detective asked a few questions. The point which seemed to interest him most concerned the pigeons.

"You're sure there was no message concealed on

the one that was shot?" he asked. "Did you look under the tail feathers?"

The boys had to admit they had not thought to look anywhere but on the legs. Probably they had missed a good clue.

Mr. Hardy could not figure out why the pigeon should have been shot down if it were on its way with a message. He asked the boys to go outside and look at the kidnaper's pigeon, which was still at their home, to compare it with the one in the woods.

The cage was being kept in the garage, and Aunt Gertrude had elected herself keeper and feeder of the bird. She went out with her nephews to show them what her good care and a well-selected diet had done for "the poor, emaciated bird" that had been delivered to them.

Suddenly Aunt Gertrude, in the lead, gave a shriek, then cried out:

"It's gone! The pigeon's gone!"

CHAPTER XVI

The Mysterious Light

THE pigeon's cage as well as the bird had disappeared. A removed pane of glass in a rear window was mute evidence of how the thief had entered the garage.

There was no question in the boys' minds as to who had taken the bird. It had to be one of Frank's kidnapers!

"But when? When?" Aunt Gertrude cried out. "I took the pigeon his supper not an hour ago."

She felt extremely annoyed over the incident, and Mr. Hardy was vexed that they had missed a second opportunity to learn who the pigeon's owner was.

"I should have followed that second pigeon to its cote. It might have helped considerably if we could have found its home. And evidently the thief thought so, too. I slipped up there, boys, and I regret my mistake."

The detective added that everything that had

happened seemed to point to the fact there was some connection between the case in which his sons had become involved, and the one involving the United States currency being stolen in foreign countries on which he was working.

"More marked bills have turned up in the U. S.," he said. "The FBI is sure the money is being used to buy something illegal in this country. They have come to no conclusion yet what it is.

"But I'll bet *you* have, Dad," Joe spoke up. "What is it?"

"Rifles."

"How did you figure that?"

The detective said his assumption was based on deduction rather than absolute proof. While in Washington he had heard about the find on the coast of one of the Central American countries of a large dory containing rifles made in the United States.

"The dory had been wrecked in a storm," the detective said, "and the men who had manned it either drowned or swam off and left it. There was no mark of identification on the boat, but I believe it came from a large vessel."

"Smugglers," Frank commented. "Dad, do you think Mr. Tyler Morton's stolen rifles are on their way to the Caribbean?"

"You've given up the idea they're in North Woods?" His father smiled.

"No, I haven't. And Joe and I want to go back there. Will you go with us?"

"Yes. But first I think we'd better take a look at the place from the air."

"You mean scout the enemy before we attack?" Joe grinned. "Let's go right away."

"The sun is too low," his father said. "There'll be deep shadows over the woods at this time of day, and we couldn't learn much. We'll go tomorrow morning."

Frank made the arrangements, and at ten o'clock next day the three Hardys were at the airport. A young man named Eric Martin, whom the boys knew, was assigned to pilot them.

"Hello," Joe said to him. "I didn't know you were a flier. Any news from Wayne?"

Eric shook his head gravely. "Not a word since that 'pirate' message."

Mr. Hardy gave the young man instructions for the reconnaissance flight, and they took off. Leaving Bayport behind, looking like a miniature waterfront town, the plane followed the Willow River, then took the tributary that headed into North Woods.

As the forest slid into view, Frank pulled binoculars from his jacket. "I see the little pond where we went swimming," he reported presently.

"That means we're close to the wolf-man's hide-out," Joe said.

"Yes, there's the pen in that clearing right below us," Frank replied. "Can't tell from this height if any wolves are in it or not."

"And there's the shack where we saw the airplane engine," Joe remarked.

The plane crisscrossed the area, but nothing suspicious came into view.

"Take her down to a thousand feet," Mr. Hardy told the pilot.

The plane banked and descended.

Frank handed the binoculars to his father, but the detective could see nothing save the dense, uneven forest below.

"Those gangsters must have some kind of camp," Joe said.

"If any of them are in North Woods," said his father, "they're taking every precaution not to have their camp spotted from the air. But I was hoping we might find something else."

"Like what?"

"Oh, smoke, a camouflaged building, trees or vegetation arranged in some significant pattern. I suppose we may as well turn back."

After the plane had landed and the Hardys were

on their way home, they made plans to leave together directly after lunch for a more careful search
through North Woods. As they walked into the
house, the detective's wife handed him a telegram.
He tore it open, read it swiftly, and frowned.

"I've been called back to Washington," he said.
"I'll have to catch a plane. This is urgent."

Mr. Hardy said he would be gone only one day.
He suggested that his sons keep busy on the case
while he was away.

"Sure, Dad. How?" Frank asked.

"Suppose you first circle the entire woodland area
in your car. It's close to seventy miles all the way
around, I'd say, and there may be another trail
that's a short cut to the thieves' camp. You'll probably find the going rough. It's pretty rugged on the
other side of North Woods."

"We've been on rough roads before." Joe grinned.

"Talk to people who live on the edge of the
woods," his father suggested. "Perhaps they can
provide you with some clues."

The brothers started out in their car after lunch,
taking the opposite direction from Black Horse Pike.
Reaching the outskirts of North Woods, the good
roads came to an end, and they began bouncing
over rutted, narrow dirt roads.

"Dad was right about this place," Frank said.
"Hope the car holds together."

They stopped at every house whose acreage bordered the woodland. Most of the farmers had no interest in the forest and knew little about it, except that a fox would sneak out now and then to kill their chickens.

About four o'clock the boys drew up beside a stooped man walking along the road. He was very friendly but tired looking, as if he had been guiding a plow all day.

"Hello, Mister," Joe greeted him. "Can we give you a ride?"

"Don't need to call me mister, son," the farmer said as he whipped out a red bandanna to wipe his forehead. "Art's the name. And thanks, but I turn down this lane."

Frank spoke of their interest in the woods. The man eyed the brothers with a skeptical half-smile.

"Stay out of them woods, boys; they ain't healthy. Why, when I was a kid like you I was helpin' my pappy loggin' in there one day, and a team and wagon sunk clean out of sight in the bogs."

The farmer sat down on a rock, pulled a stem of grass, put it between his teeth, and went on with his warning.

"Them woods is a good place to stay clear of, I always tell folks. Why, out yonder there's a pit full of snakes; hundreds of 'em wrigglin' around like they was crazy."

Frank and Joe looked at each other as the man continued, "Then there's those wild dogs, too. Ain't never seen 'em, but on clear nights I hear 'em."

"Anybody live in North Woods?" Frank asked.

"Not that I ever heerd tell of, son."

The boys thanked the farmer and drove on to the next place. They found its owner as full of wild tales as his neighbor. He had been told that any humans or farm animals straying into the forest were never seen alive again, though their cries of agony could be heard for miles.

"Did you ever hear any?" Frank asked.

"No. But I once did hear a siren—like a fire-engine siren—and right after that there was a glow over the trees, just like the Northern Lights."

This man was sure no one lived in the forest any longer. The whole tract had been bought up by a lumber company years before, he told them. There were rumors that strangers had been seen on one of the old woods road; surveyors, most likely. The boys drove off, excited by what they had heard.

"What do you think of that siren and light story, Frank?"

"If we hadn't heard the siren ourselves, and seen the wolves, I'd say all the stories were farfetched yarns. I'm sure the wild-dog rumor was circulated by people who want to keep visitors out of North Woods."

Joe was all for going into the forest at once and having another look at the wolf-man's place.

Frank shook his head. "Nobody'd know where we were. And, anyway, an order from Dad is—"

"You're right. Let's finish our job."

The boys made a complete circuit of the forest, but found no trails that looked as though they had recently been used. The only new clue the day had yielded was the matter of the unexplained lights. Both boys were puzzled to find an explanation of what they could be.

"Joe, if you'll remember, it's the second time there's been a connection between a sudden flash of lights and a wailing siren," Frank said. "Do you suppose the one that night on the ocean, when every light on the yacht suddenly blazed up, could have anything to do with the lights and the siren in North Woods?"

Joe grinned. "You're stretching my imagination, but you probably mean that the plane could have signaled and the lights were an answer both times?"

"Exactly. When the siren wailed over North Woods, we weren't close enough and the trees were too thick for us to see any lights."

"But we didn't hear a plane."

"That's correct! So we're right back where we started from, which is exactly nowhere."

Frank switched on the car radio, hoping for good news of Jack Wayne. But again the report was disappointing, and the announcer said hope for the flier was waning. The Hardys drove the rest of the way home in silence.

Frank pulled into the driveway and drove the car into the garage. He and Joe jumped out and made for the back steps, but the door swung open before they had reached it. Out came Mrs. Hardy, obivously agitated.

"Frank! Joe!" she cried. "I'm so glad you're back."

"What's the matter, Mother?"

"It's Chet. He's been telephoning every few minutes for the past half-hour."

"Why?"

"He's in trouble. Needs your help right away!"

CHAPTER XVII

An Urgent Plea

CHET in trouble again!

"Did he say what about?" Joe asked.

Mrs. Hardy shook her head. "But he wants you to go right over to the farm."

"I wonder if it has anything to do with the stolen rifles," Frank mused.

"We'll soon find out," Joe replied as he ran back toward the garage with Frank a few strides behind him.

"Just a minute," their mother called.

She said one of them was to go to the hotel where Mr. Hardy's operative Sam Radley was waiting for some letters that had come to the house for him from Washington. And the detective had something that he wanted brought back. Mrs. Hardy could not leave because her husband had said he would telephone again from Washington. Aunt Gertrude was out.

"I'll do it," Frank offered. "Joe, you go to Chet's. I'll be back here in twenty minutes. If you need any reinforcements out at the Mortons', call me."

When Frank returned from the errand, he found his mother even more disturbed than before.

"Chet phoned again," she said. "He told me what the trouble is. Actually, it's a family matter. Chet says they must have two thousand five hundred dollars tonight. Mr. Morton is away on business for the Dairymen's League and Chet says his mother begs us to lend her at least two thousand dollars of it until he comes home. The banks are open this evening. Chet will drive over for the money in three-quarters of an hour. Poor boy, he was so confused he could hardly talk."

"Did you talk to Mrs. Morton herself, Mother?" Frank asked.

"No, dear," she replied. "Chet said she couldn't come to the telephone."

"Mother, you didn't fall for a line like that!" Frank exclaimed. "Chet's mother would never ask for a loan of that much money!"

Mrs. Hardy looked at her tall son in amazement as he continued.

"The person who will call for the money will be the one who lost the two thousand dollars we found. This is our chance to catch him!"

Mrs. Hardy was unconvinced. Despite the fact that she had utmost confidence in Frank's judgment, she was the type of woman, when a friend was in need, who would make any sacrifice to help. Besides, she was sure the voice on the telephone had been Chet Morton's. And Chet would not delibately deceive her.

"It's something to do with a relative. Chet did not seem to want to explain, and I got the feeling from his being so upset that the Mortons didn't care to tell us why they needed the money."

"All right," her son said, putting an arm around his mother's shoulder. "I know you're generous and sympathetic, but we can easily check on Chet's story. I'm going to telephone Joe. He should be at the Mortons' by this time."

He quickly dialed Chet's number. It was several seconds before the boy picked up the receiver.

"Hello? Frank?"

"Is Joe there? Put him on."

"Y-yes."

"Say, Joe, what's the story about the two thousand five hundred dollars? It's not a phony?"

"It isn't phony," Joe replied. "I believe we ought to lend the Mortons the money."

"What! Where's Mrs. Morton?"

"Out. She's getting the other five hundred dollars."

"You really think we should do this?" Frank asked.

"Yes."

The older boy hesitated. He regretted that he and Joe had not arranged a new code, so Joe could signal if everything were not aboveboard. The Hardys made it a rule never to use the same code twice on a case, so Frank refrained from saying, "We were just going to take Mother to the doctor," as his father had said to him at the time of the kidnaping.

Instead, Frank told Joe he would get the two thousand dollars. "Tell Chet I'll bring it out."

"No, don't do that," Joe replied. "Chet will pick it up."

"You're coming, too?"

"Sure."

Frank hung up. He was perplexed. Maybe the deal was on the level, after all.

As a result of the conversation, Mrs. Hardy hastened to her desk in the corner of the living room. She drew out her savings account book, and wrote a withdrawal slip for the amount—two thousand dollars.

Her son put the book and slip in his pocket, and hurried down the street. "I have an uneasy feeling about this whole deal," he told himself as he arrived at the bank. "I hope Joe hasn't been fooled."

He pushed through the revolving door and laid the book and slip on a teller's counter. When the clerk looked up and recognized Frank, he lifted his eyebrows.

"How do you want this?" he asked.

"Give it to me in twenty-dollar bills, please," Frank said. "And list the serial numbers, will you?"

The teller glanced at Frank with a smile. "This is a departure from your usual mysteries, isn't it, Frank? You're usually on the collecting end instead of the pay-off end."

Frank nodded. The teller listed the numbers and gave the boy a duplicate. Then he stamped the bankbook and handed Frank the money. As he started home, Frank suddenly remembered the night he had been attacked and kidnaped on his way to the ball park. With such a large sum of money on his person he should not risk a holdup.

The serial numbers of the bills had been his first precaution. Now he would stop at police headquarters and ask for a ride home. He was tempted to tell Chief Collig his suspicions, but decided this might embarrass the Mortons. It would be better to call upon Biff and Tony to carry out the next part of his plan.

Arriving home in the police car, he telephoned first one, then the other. He asked them to drive at once to the road that led past the Morton farm.

When Chet and Joe left there, they were to warn the boys if anyone followed them. In any case, Biff and Tony were to keep an eye on Chet until he got home again.

The boys readily agreed, eager to take part in a new adventure. Tony said he would start at once in his car and pick up Biff.

To Frank, the next half-hour ticked by as if every second were a day. He breathed a sigh of relief when the stutter of Chet's jalopy told him the boy was only a block away. Frank rushed to the curb, the envelope with the money in his pocket.

The car made its way erratically down the street, weaving as if the driver were not in full control of his faculties. Chet stopped the car and stared at Frank as if he had never seen him before. His round, full face was damp with perspiration, and his eyes revealed a terrible fear that made his hands tremble on the wheel.

"What's the matter, Chet? Is the trouble bad?" Frank asked. "Come inside and we'll talk it over."

"No-no," Chet pleaded. "Give me the money and let me get back home as quick as I can."

"Where's Joe?"

Chet did not reply for a second, then he whispered, "He-he's coming."

"Can't you stop in for a minute? I'd like to ask you a few questions."

Chet's double chin quivered as he gulped. His mouth was so dry he could hardly rasp out, "Please, please, Frank. No. No. I tell you I have to go. Give me the money."

When Frank drew the envelope from his pocket, Chet snatched it from his hand.

"Chet, you . . ."

"Good-by!" the frightened boy fairly squealed. The old car lurched forward and rumbled down the street.

As he entered the house again, Frank realized that Chet must be in a terrible state of shock brought about by severe worry. How serious was the Morton trouble? Maybe Joe would be able to tell him when he came.

After twenty minutes went by and his brother still had not returned, Frank became anxious.

"I'll phone the farm," he decided. Mrs. Morton answered the ring.

"This is Frank. Is Joe there?"

"Why, no," came the reply. "I haven't seen him."

"Is Chet home yet?"

"No."

"Well, he has the money," Frank said.

"Money?" Mrs. Morton's voice sounded casual.

"I mean the money you asked for. I gave it to Chet."

There was silence for a moment. "I don't understand, Frank. I didn't ask for any money."

The boy groaned. His hunch had been right. What he had suspected might be a swindle had turned out to be one. What a fool he had been! And what had happened to Chet and Joe?

CHAPTER XVIII

Two Knockouts

SINCE Mrs. Morton knew nothing about the strange request for two thousand five hundred dollars, Frank decided he had better not alarm her before investigating further. Drawing in a deep breath, he said:

"When you see Chet or Joe, will you have them get in touch with me right away, Mrs. Morton?"

"Yes, Frank. But what about the money?"

"Chet can explain that better than I can," Frank replied. He said good-by and hung up.

Mrs. Hardy overheard the conversation and immediately became alarmed. Her son's face wore a grim look. He tried to reassure her that the money was safe.

"Oh, why didn't I listen to you? I've been so gullible," she said tearfully.

Frank's next move was to contact Biff and Tony. Perhaps they had the explanation. Frank's hands